Publisher
MIKE RICHARDSON

Series Editor
DIANA SCHUTZ

Collection Editor
CHRIS WARNER

Collection Designer
CARY GRAZZINI

This book collects issues 23–30
of the Dark Horse comic-book series *Usagi Yojimbo™ Volume Three.*

Visit the Usagi Dojo website
www.usagiyojimbo.com

Published by
Dark Horse Comics, Inc.
10956 SE Main Street
Milwaukie, OR 97222

www.darkhorse.com

To find a comics shop in your area,
call the Comic Shop Locator Service toll-free at 1-888-266-4226

First edition: March 2000
ISBN: 1-56971-459-2

3 5 7 9 10 8 6 4 2
Printed in Canada

— Grey Shadows —

Created, Written,
and Illustrated by

Stan Sakai

Introduction by

Max Allan Collins

Usagi Yojimbo

The Case Of Usagi Yojimbo

I AM GRATEFUL to Stan Sakai for a number of reasons.

First, and foremost, he has created one of the best and longest-running independent comic-book series in the history of the medium.

Second, he has been nice enough to acknowledge me, in the story notes for "The Hairpin Murders," as one of his two favorite mystery writers. (His other favorite is Ed McBain, whose 87th Precinct novels I have followed since I was about the age that my son Nathan discovered *Usagi Yojimbo*.)

And, finally, Stan Sakai did the impossible: he (however briefly) managed to make my teenage son impressed with his old man.

Stan Sakai is Nate's favorite cartoonist, and *Usagi Yojimbo* is his favorite comic book. None of this is surprising, because Stan's work is about as good as current comics get, and Nate was raised on a steady diet of *Lone Wolf and Cub* manga, John Woo movies, and Japanese video games.

For my entire life (short as it may be), I have been a great fan of comics. Living with a writer of comics made it inevitable: I grew up on everything from Teenage Mutant Ninja Turtles *to* Calvin And Hobbes. *But at the tender age of eleven, I was subjected by my father to a different type of comic book — the manga. After I had read graphic novels like* Barefoot Gen *and the* Lone Wolf and Cub *series, my father steered me to* Usagi Yojimbo.

These brief moments of respect I receive from Nate — however fleeting — have occurred at comics conventions when we have approached Stan, to get copies of Nate's *Usagi* comics signed. And, invariably, inevitably, Stan lights up, seeing me, and informs Nate and me that he — the creator of *Usagi Yojimbo*! — has brought books of mine to have me sign.

This admiration of course bewilders my son, but somewhere in the confusion is a stirring notion that his father may have some value...after all, Stan Sakai approves.

Which is fine with me, because I sure approve of Stan Sakai. Having worked, off and on, in this field since the late '70s, I've become pretty jaded and little impresses me, particularly new stuff. But Stan Sakai is an exception: he stirs in me memories of the classic comic strips, where the likes of Dick Tracy and Little Orphan Annie and Wash Tubbs could — despite their cartoony depictions — enjoy thrilling adventures. His "funny animal" approach invokes the great Carl Barks guiding Uncle Scrooge through journeys of mystery and excitement, in exotic settings, thrilling tales that dared not to be terribly funny...just terrific. His boyish yet courageous Usagi summons the ghost of Herge's Tintin, that kid reporter whose exploits managed to have a childlike innocence while being extremely adult.

I quickly became addicted to the cute rabbit and his adventures. I was drawn in by many aspects of the comic: the beautiful artwork, so detailed and simple at the same time; the Japanese culture and mythology, with demons, ninja, and sword fights; and the rich story lines that held it all together, stories that brought alive Japanese folklore to an audience that would never have seen it otherwise...and fueled my interest in Japanese culture.

Stan Sakai has written and drawn a series that both Nate and I can read — and that Nate has been able to keep reading as he grows to adulthood.

In the stories in this book, Stan introduces one of his best characters — Inspector Ishida — who shares the same real-life role model as Charlie Chan: Honolulu detective Chang Apana. Ishida — who spouts wisdom in a vaguely Chan-like manner — is more like the hardboiled Apana than the mild-mannered Chan of Earl Derr Biggers' novels (and the many films they spawned). Ishida is an action hero, and Usagi makes a great, sword-slinging Watson for him in mystery yarns that are involving, exciting, and deftly plotted.

Besides being an expert storyteller and artist, Stan Sakai is a genuinely kind man. He has always been very nice and personable to me and the rest of his fans I have met at various conventions. Stan Sakai deserves every bit of praise and respect that he has received, and I have no doubt that after reading this collection, you would agree with me.

MAX ALLAN COLLINS (WITH *NATHAN COLLINS*)

Max Allan Collins is the author of the Shamus Award winning Nathan Heller novels (including Damned In Paradise, *in which Chang Apana appears), and his comics scripting includes the* Dick Tracy *comic strip (1977-1993),* Ms. Tree, Batman, Johnny Dynamite, *and the acclaimed graphic novel* Road To Perdition. *Nathan Collins is a seventeen-year-old high school student whose interests include band, computer games, and* Usagi Yojimbo. *He has appeared as an actor in three independent features directed by his father.*

Contents

For Don Dougherty,
one of my oldest and dearest friends,
and for Marcia, Kendall, and Evan

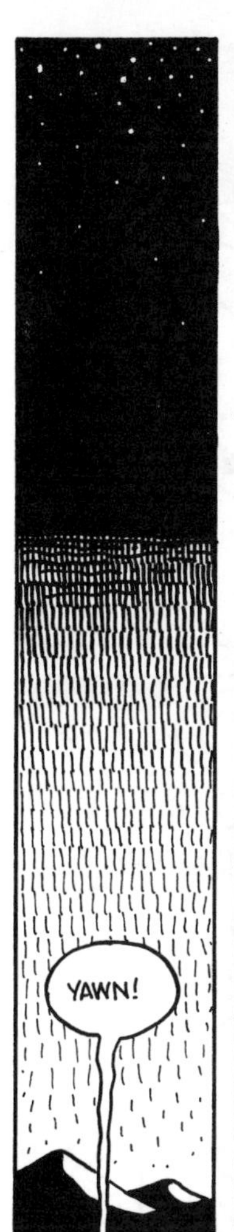
YAWN!

MY FATHER'S SWORDS
HO-HUM... SMACK! SMACK!
MUMBLE! MUMBLE!

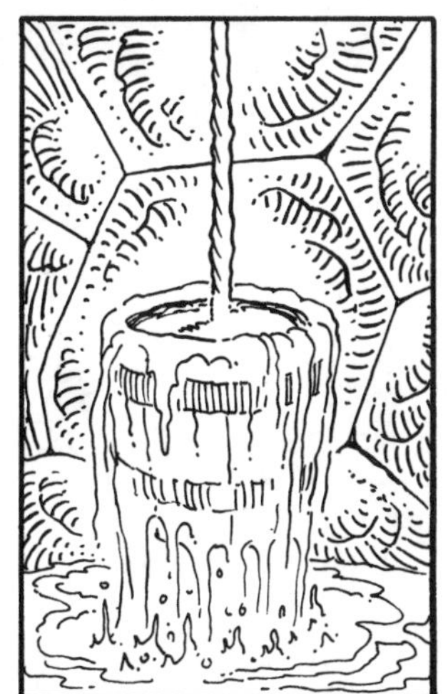

1.

SCRUB!
SCRUB!
SIP! SIP! SWISH! SWISH!
SPIT!
BLURGG! GLURKK!
SPLASH! SPLASH!
WIPE! WIPE!
AH...
CRAK!
GOOD MORNING, USAGI!

AH, PRIEST SANSHOBO! WELCOME BACK!
THANK YOU, MY FRIEND!
HOW ARE YOU TODAY?

MUCH BETTER. MY ARM IS HEALING NICELY-- SEE?
BUT I AM CONCERNED ABOUT GEN.

IT'S BEEN A WEEK AND HIS RECOVERY IS STEADY...BUT SLOW.
HMM...

IT SEEMED A CLEAN SPEAR WOUND, NOT VERY SERIOUS.
IS THE WOUND FESTERING?
THERE WAS NOTHING CLEAN ABOUT THE WEAPON ...OR ITS WIELDER!

IT'S MORE THAN THE WOUND. IT'S AS IF HE HAD BEEN... *DRAINED.*
LET US CHECK IN ON HIM.
WELCOME BACK, HEAD PRIEST.

HOW IS YOUR PATIENT TODAY, SENZO?
HIS RECOVERY WOULD BE QUICKER IF HE WEREN'T SO MELANCHOLY. IT'S ALMOST AS IF HE NEEDS A REASON TO LIVE.
3.

GOOD MORNING, GEN.
THIS IS SANSHOBO, HEAD PRIEST OF THIS TEMPLE.
I HAVE JUST RETURNED FROM REPORTING THE DEATHS OF MY PRIESTS.
AN UGLY TASK.
ER... I'M OBLIGED FOR YOUR HOSPITALITY.

USAGI IS A GOOD FRIEND. MY WELCOME EXTENDS TO ALL OF HIS FRIENDS.

IN RETURN, ALL I ASK IS THAT YOU GET WELL.
HRMMPH!
ER... WHAT DID THE AUTHORITIES SAY, SANSHOBO?

THEY DON'T KNOW WHAT TO MAKE OF THE SLAIN PRIESTS, BUT THEIR EFFORTS ARE ELSEWHERE.
THERE HAS BEEN A RASH OF KILLINGS LATELY... MANY OF WHICH, I SUSPECT, ARE RELATED TO THAT SWORD, GRASSCUTTER.

LORD SAKANA-NO-ASHIYUBI WAS KILLED, AND THE CULPRIT SOUNDS LIKE THE ONE YOU CALL JEI. SO, YOU SEE, THE DEATH OF SOME MENDICANT PRIESTS RATES A LOW PRIORITY.
4.

EVEN THE GEISHU LORD WAS ALMOST ASSASSINATED.
LORD NORIYUKI?!
WHAT HAPPENED?

I HEARD THERE WAS A TRAITOR WITHIN THE CLAN WHO HAS SINCE BEEN SLAIN... THOUGH THERE ARE RUMORS OF A GREATER CONSPIRACY.
WHAT OF THE WOMAN, TOMOE?
THAT IS ALL I KNOW.

YOU APPEAR CONCERNED.
THEY ARE-- FRIENDS.

THEN PERHAPS LORD NORIYUKI SHOULD GAIN CUSTODY OF THE SWORD OF THE GODS.
BUT HE IS LOYAL TO THE SHOGUNATE AND SO WILL DELIVER THE BLADE TO THE MILITARY LEADER.

I THINK YOUR ORIGINAL PLAN IS STILL THE BEST-- TO REPLACE THE TRUE SWORD WITH THE COUNTERFEIT THAT IS KEPT AT ATSUTA SHRINE.
5

THEN IT'S AGREED. I WILL TAKE THE SWORD TO ATSUTA ONCE THINGS QUIET DOWN AROUND HERE.
SANSHOBO...

LET ME ACCOMPANY YOU ONCE I'VE RECOVERED. I'VE SEEN IT THROUGH THIS FAR-- I MAY AS WELL GO ON TO THE END.

OF COURSE, GEN! I WOULD WELCOME YOUR COMPANY.
THAT SEEMS TO HAVE SNAPPED YOU OUT OF YOUR MELANCHOLY!
HRMPH!

COUNT ME IN ON THIS ADVENTURE AS WELL.
OF COURSE!

BUT IF THE TURMOIL IN THE AREA IS AS YOU SAY, I WOULD FIRST LIKE TO CHECK OUT THE SITUATION FOR MYSELF.
I WANT NO MORE SURPRISES!

THAT MAY BE A WISE PRECAUTION.
I SHOULD BE BACK IN A FEW WEEKS.
6.

TAKE CARE OF YOURSELF, USAGI.
HERE'S THE RECEIPT FOR THE OUTLAW HOSOKU'S BOUNTY. I'LL BE HERE FOR A WHILE, SO COLLECT IT FOR ME.
SURE. I'LL NEED SOME TRAVELING MONEY.
WHAT?!

THAT'S MY MONEY, LONG-EARS!
YOU'D BETTER COME BACK WITH ALL OF IT!
SEE YOU IN A FEW WEEKS!
I'M GOING TO COUNT EVERY COPPER ZENI*!
IF IT'S NOT ALL THERE, YOU'LL BE SORRY!
IF THIS DOESN'T GIVE HIM A REASON FOR LIVING, NOTHING WILL.
*SMALL COIN

THIS LOOKS LIKE THE AREA THAT SANSHOBO DESCRIBED.
7

NO BODY...

JUST HIS SPEAR...

THE DEMON'S SPEAR!

HIYAHH!
CHOP!

8.

WHAT'S GOING ON?
A MATCH.
TCH! THESE SAMURAI ARE FOOLS WITH NOTHING BETTER TO DO THAN SHOW OFF THEIR SKILLS.
THEY'RE ALL IDIOTS!
TCH!
9.

THAT SPEARMAN LOOKS FIERCE! THE KID HAS NO CHANCE AGAINST HIM!
THE BOY WILL WIN.

OH, YEAH?! HOW ABOUT A WAGER, THEN? I'VE GOT TEN ZENI!
IF YOU INSIST.

HIYAAHH!
C'MON, SPEAR-GUY, C'MON!

KONK!

GRUMBLE! GRUMBLE!

GRUMBLE! GRUMBLE! MUMBLE!

10.

CONGRATULATIONS.
THANK YOU. I WAS LUCKY.
NONSENSE.

YOUR TECHNIQUE LOOKED FAMILIAR... AND SO DO YOUR SWORDS.
I AM DONBORI CHIAKI. THESE SWORDS BELONGED TO MY FATHER.

DONBORI MATSUO AND I SERVED UNDER LORD MIFUNE.
YOU KNEW MY FATHER?!

HE WAS A FINE SAMURAI. HE SAVED MY LIFE.

"IT WAS DURING THE BATTLE OF THE BURNING PLAINS, ONE OF THE LESSER SKIRMISHES BUT BLOODY NO LESS. HE AND I WERE IN PURSUIT OF A FLEEING BAND OF DARK SUN WARRIORS..."
11.

SUDDENLY...
ARCHERS!
WHINNY!
IT'S A TRAP!
UH--!
FWITT!
FWITT!
FWITT!
FWITT!
FWITT
FWITT!
FWITT!
FWITT!
FWITT!
FWITT!
THUK!
THUK!
THUK!
THUK!
THUK!
USAGI!
MATSUO-- GET OUT OF HERE!
GRAB MY HAND!
"I WOULD SURELY HAVE BEEN SLAIN IF IT HAD NOT BEEN FOR YOUR FATHER."

"USAGI"? YOU ARE MIYAMOTO USAGI?! AH, MANY TIMES HAVE I HEARD MY FATHER SPEAK OF YOU. HE VALUED YOUR FRIENDSHIP!
HE WAS A GOOD FRIEND AND A FINE WARRIOR. I WAS SADDENED TO LEARN OF HIS DEATH AT THE BATTLE OF ADACHI PLAIN.
HE WAS A GREAT SAMURAI, ONE WHOSE DEEDS I ASPIRE TO.
YOU REMIND ME MUCH OF YOUR FATHER.
I TRAVEL THE WARRIOR PILGRIMAGE, HONING MY SKILLS TO HONOR HIM...
...THOUGH IT WILL BE DIFFICULT TO LIVE UP TO HIS LEGEND.
YOU COULD HAVE NO FINER ROLE MODEL.
HE IS A WORTHY SON.
HE IS DETERMINED TO BRING HONOR TO HIS FATHER'S MEMORY. EXPERIENCE WILL IMPROVE HIS SWORDSMANSHIP, BUT HE ALREADY HAS THE SPIRIT OF BUSHIDO*.
*"THE WARRIOR'S WAY"
13

LATER...
...AND YOUR FATHER AND I HAD TO DRESS IN WOMEN'S CLOTHING TO SNEAK BACK INTO THE CASTLE!
HA HA HA HA!
GLUB! GLUB!
BURP! BAH! EMPTY!

YOU DARE TO SOIL MY SWORD?!
YOUR FILTHY GARMENT TOUCHED MY SCABBARD--THE GUARDIAN OF MY SOUL! SUCH AN AFFRONT CAN ONLY BE PARDONED WITH YOUR LIFE!
STAND STILL, YOU! HIC!
SWISH!

WHAT'S GOING ON HERE?
BAH! THIS IS NOT YOUR CONCERN! GO AWAY!
YOU'RE DRUNK!
GO AWAY, I SAID! THIS IS MY BUSINESS!

YOU NEED NOT BULLY THOSE LESS FORTUNATE THAN YOU! IT IS NOT A SAMURAI'S WAY!
14

WHAT DO YOU KNOW OF BEING A SAMURAI, YOU-- YOU YOUNG WHELP?!
YOU WANNA FIGHT ME?!
HUH?!
I DON'T WANT ANY TROUBLE. BESIDES, YOU'RE DRUNK. YOU CAN BARELY WALK, MUCH LESS FIGHT.

SPUT! SPUT! WHA--?! DRUNK?! ME?! WHY, YOU--! I CAN STILL TAKE ON THE LIKES OF YOU!

HIYAHH!!

WUMPH!

OOOOOOOH...
IT DISGUSTS ME THAT A SAMURAI COULD ACT SO.
HEY, WHERE DID THAT GUY GO?
15

I THOUGHT HE'D AT LEAST STAY TO THANK US... MAYBE WE COULD HELP HIM.
PEOPLE LIKE HIM TEND TO BE INVISIBLE.
NO, WE ONLY TREAT THEM THAT WAY.
SOON...
WELL, MY WAY TAKES ME EAST THROUGH THE MOUNTAIN PASS.
AND MY ROAD IS TO THE NORTH.
I HOPE YOU FIND WHAT YOU SEARCH FOR, CHIAKI.
AS DO YOU, USAGI-SAN.
A FINE YOUNG MAN.
I HOPE OUR PATHS CROSS AGAIN SOMEDAY.
16.

SOMEONE IS COMING!
WHAT CAN ONE SO YOUNG DO AGAINST ALL OF US?
HE'LL PROBABLY GIVE UP HIS MONEY WITHOUT EVEN A FIGHT!
YEAH, BUT HE'S A SAMURAI!
YEAH. DEEP DOWN THESE SAMURAI ARE A COWARDLY LOT!

LOOK AT HIS CLOTHES. HE LOOKS LIKE HE CARRIES A HEAVY PURSE...
...OR WOULD YOU BE CONTENT WITH THOSE PEASANTS WHO HAVE BEEN PASSING BY?
YEAH. YOU'RE RIGHT!

UP THE RIVER, ALONG THE MOUNTAIN TRAIL...
BRIGANDS LYING IN WAIT! CHIAKI IS IN DANGER!
CHIAKI-- BE ALERT!
WHAT?!

HIIIYAHHH!!!
WE JUST WANT YOUR PURSE! TOSS IT OVER AND CONTINUE ON YOUR WAY!
17

IF YOU WANT MY PURSE, YOU'LL HAVE TO TAKE IT!
LOOK OUT FOR HIS SWORD!
CIRCLE AROUND HIM! GET BEHIND HIM!

CHIAKI!

KLOP
KLOP
KLOP
KLOP

THUD!
18

OWW! HE CUT ME, THAT DIRTY GRUB!
YOU CAME OFF LUCKY! POOR HANTO IS DEAD!
HURRY! SOMEONE IS COMING!
TOO LATE! KILL THIS ONE QUICKLY AND TAKE HIS PURSE!
GRAB HIS SWORDS, TOO!

HIYAHHA!!
WHAT?!
!
?

KONK!
OWW!
WHO IS HE?!
IT'S JUST SOME CRIPPLE!
KILL HIM!

19.

YAHH!

GYARK!

PHLOO!

EYUGH!
WHA--?

CHIAKI!
HE'S ALL RIGHT--JUST UNCONSCIOUS.
THANK THE GODS!
20.

HE OWES YOU HIS LIFE...
...BUT WHO ARE YOU?
EH?
YOU FAIL TO RECOGNIZE ME, USAGI?
I-I KNOW YOU?
SURELY YOU MUST REMEMBER AN OLD COMRADE!
"COMRADE"?
NO--! IT CAN'T BE!
YOU WERE LEFT FOR DEAD AT ADACHI PLAIN!
AHEH! SO I WAS TOLD.
21.

YOU HAVE BEEN FOLLOWING YOUR SON WITHOUT HIS KNOWLEDGE.
YES. HE IS A GOOD AND HONORABLE SAMURAI. HE DOES ME PROUD.

WHY NOT REVEAL YOURSELF TO HIM? HE WOULD REJOICE TO FIND YOU'RE STILL ALIVE!
NO!

ALL THAT HE HAS ACCOMPLISHED, HE DID FOR MY MEMORY'S SAKE.

LET HIM LOVE AND REVERE THE LEGEND, AND LET MY BONES LIE BURIED AT ADACHI PLAIN.
YOU ARE HIS FATHER. HE WILL HONOR YOU!
HE HONORS ME NOW.

HE MUST NOT KNOW THAT I STILL LIVE.
I-I DON'T UNDERSTAND.

MY ARM... MY EYE... LOST AT ADACHI PLAIN. MY BODY WAS TRAMPLED OVER BY HIKIJI'S HORSES. I SHOULD HAVE DIED THERE, AND SOMETIMES I WISH I HAD. BUT MY DEATH HAD GIVEN INSPIRATION TO MY SON AND SET HIM ON THE ROAD TO BUSHIDO. IT IS THE LEGEND THAT HE FOLLOWS-- NOT THE MAN. HE MUST NOT SEE ME NOW, A PARODY OF WHAT I ONCE WAS. THE GODS HAVE GIVEN ME MY LIFE AS A GIFT SO I CAN SEE CHIAKI FOLLOW THE ROAD WITH HIS FATHER, THE WARRIOR, AS HIS GUIDE. YOU CANNOT TAKE THAT AWAY FROM US!
22.

I SAVED YOUR LIFE AT THE BURNING PLAINS, USAGI. YOU OWE ME A DEBT!
.....
YOU CANNOT TELL HIM I YET LIVE!
BUT IT'S WRONG! YOU CAN'T HOLD ME TO SUCH A REQUEST!

UHH...

CHIAKI, YOU'RE SAFE NOW. TAKE IT CAREFULLY!
UHH...

WHAT--? USAGI-SAN?
OW, MY HEAD.
YOU SAVED ME. I OWE YOU MY LIFE!
NO. IT WAS--
23.

IT WAS...
WHAT IS IT, USAGI-SAN?
UH...

IT WAS JUST A CHANCE TO REPAY AN OLD DEBT.

THE END.

UHH--!
THUD!
I'M FAR FROM THE VILLAGE... I PRAY I'M SAFE NOW!
¡GASP!¡
I-I HEAR MUSIC--FAR AWAY BUT GETTING CLOSER!

IT'S NOT SAFE, EVEN IN THE LIGHT OF DAY!
THE MUSIC IS GETTING LOUDER!
AND IT'S GETTING DARKER!
ULP!
OW!
NO!
NO!
NO!
2.

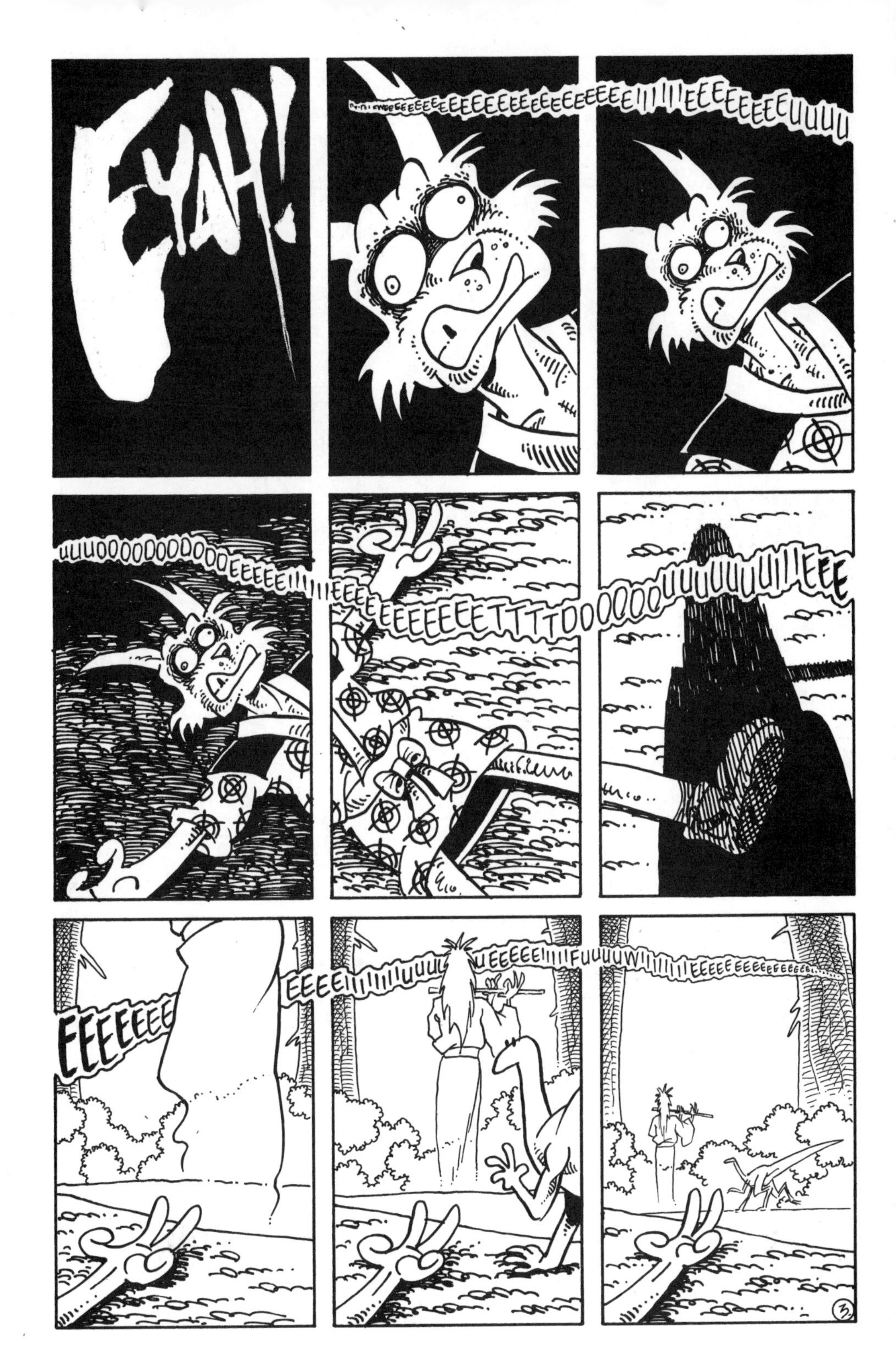
EYAH!
EEEEEEEEEEEEEEEEEEEEEE!!!!!EEEEEEEEEUUUU
UUUOOOOOOOOOOOEEEEEE!!!!!EEEEEEEEEEETTTTOOOOOOOUUUUUUU!!EEE
EEEEEEE
EEEE!!!!!UUUUUEEEEEE!!!!FUUUW!!!!!EEEEEEEEE

FFFWW

EH?

IT SOUNDS LIKE THERE'S ANOTHER FLUTE PLAYER IN THE AREA.

SUCH A STRANGE, HAUNTING TUNE.
PERHAPS HE'LL TEACH IT TO ME.

IT'S COMING FROM THIS DIRECTION.
EH?
RUSTLE! RUSTLE!

A *WHITE* *TOKAGE´*!
I'VE NEVER SEEN SUCH A CREATURE BEFORE!
EEP!

THE MUSIC IS FADING!

BUT IT SEEMED TO COME FROM *THIS* WAY--THE DIRECTION THE *TOKAGE´* WAS RUNNING!

A SMALL FARMING VILLAGE... COULD SUCH AN ARTISTIC SOUL BELONG TO ONE WHO LABORS ALL DAY IN THE FIELDS?
5

A STRANGER! A STRANGER APPROACHES!

THE DEMON FLUTE
STRANGE. USUALLY FARMERS IN THESE OUTLYING VILLAGES ARE SO FRIENDLY.
THERE IS MUCH FEAR HERE.
LOOK-- HE HAS A FLUTE!
H-HE MUST BE THE MONSTER!
6.

I AM FRIEND TO SANSHOBO AND THE PRIESTS OF THIS AREA! WHAT IS WRONG?
HEAD PRIEST SANSHOBO?
D-DID HIRO SEND YOU, SAMURAI?
THEN...HE MADE IT OUT OKAY?

I'M SORRY. I DON'T KNOW WHAT YOU'RE TALKING ABOUT.
WE'LL TAKE YOU TO THE HEAD MAN. HE'LL EXPLAIN EVERYTHING TO YOU!

LAST NIGHT OUR VILLAGE SUFFERED A SERIES OF MURDERS, USAGI-SAN.
HOW WERE THE VICTIMS KILLED?
WE DON'T KNOW.
THERE WERE NO WITNESSES?
7.

THERE WERE **MANY** WITNESSES TO THE CRIME, BUT NO ONE SAW ANYTHING!
I DON'T UNDERSTAND.

LET ME START FROM THE BEGINNING. FOR THE PAST FEW DAYS WE'VE BEEN HEARING THE HAUNTING MELODY OF A FLUTE. AT FIRST IT SOUNDED DISTANT, BUT EACH DAY IT WAS CLOSER, CLEARER.

WE PAID IT LITTLE HEED, MERELY ASSUMING IT WAS A STRANGER PLAYING HIS FLUTE IN THE MOUNTAINS.

"LAST NIGHT THE MUSIC WAS THE CLEAREST IT HAS EVER BEEN. IN FACT, MANY OF US SAT OUTSIDE OUR HOMES ENJOYING THE MELODY.

"THEN, IN SPITE OF THE FULL MOON, IT GREW DARKER AND DARKER, AS IF WE WERE ENVELOPED BY A BLACK CLOUD.

"THEN THE SCREAMS...
EEEEEE--!
GYAAAHHH!
YAGGGHH!
8.

"A FEW SECONDS LATER THE MIST LIFTED, AND THERE ON THE GROUND LAY THREE OF OUR NEIGHBORS, DEAD.
"THEY WERE HORRIBLY MUTILATED-- AS IF CLAWED BY SOME SAVAGE BEAST!

"WE HEARD THE SOUNDS OF THE FLUTE AGAIN AND SAW ITS PLAYER--A GAUNT FIGURE FOLLOWED BY A WHITE TOKAGE"!

"THEY SOON DISAPPEARED INTO THE NIGHT, AND NO ONE HAD THE BRAVERY TO PURSUE THEM.

"WE HUDDLED IN OUR HOMES UNTIL MORNING WHEN HIRO VOLUNTEERED TO GO OUT AND REPORT THE MURDERS."

BUT THE NIGHT IS APPROACHING, AND ONCE AGAIN WE HAVE CAUSE TO FEAR THE GAUNT FIGURE IN WHITE!
9.

IN TODAY'S LIGHT I HEARD THE FLUTE AND SAW THE WHITE *TOKAGE*. THEY LED ME TO YOUR VILLAGE.
GASP! SO THEY DO NOT ONLY BELONG TO THE NIGHT!
THOUGH MAYBE THEY DO NOT KILL DURING THE DAY!

THEY MUST HAVE LURED YOU HERE TO SLAY YOU AS WE WILL BE SLAIN!

HOW FAR IS IT TO THE NEXT VILLAGE?
A HALF DAY'S TRAVEL.

THEN WE MUST HOPE HIRO IS THERE NOW AND WAIT FOR HELP TO ARRIVE IN THE MORNING.
B-BUT WHAT OF TONIGHT?

LIGHT TORCHES THROUGHOUT THE VILLAGE. EVERYONE SHOULD STAY LOCKED WITHIN THEIR OWN HOMES.

WHAT OF YOU, USAGI-SAN?
I'LL BE OUTSIDE. I WILL CONFRONT THIS MYSTERIOUS SPECTER.
SIP!
10.

SO COLD... DESPITE THE FIRES.

CRIK!
HUH!

EEP!
A GREEN TOKAGE!
WHEW!

HOURS PASS...

AND MORE HOURS...
IT'S NEARLY THE HOUR OF THE OX*-WHEN OBAKE* ARE MOST ACTIVE.
* 2-4 A.M.
** HAUNTS

A FLUTE--!
--DISTANT BUT GETTING LOUDER!
11.

A-A CLOUD OF DARKNESS CREEPING TOWARDS ME...

WHO'S THERE?

STOP! WHAT ARE YOU?!

THE MUSIC IS GETTING LOUDER! IT'S ALMOST DEAFENING!

12

TH-THE DARK IS RETREATING...
...AND THE MUSIC IS FADING!

I-IT'S GONE AWAY-- *WHEW!* M-MY HANDS ARE SHAKING AND I'VE BROKEN OUT WITH *TORIHADA**!
*GOOSEBUMPS (LITERALLY "CHICKEN SKIN")

EEEEEEE
WHAT?!

IT CAME FROM THE HEAD MAN'S HOUSE!
13

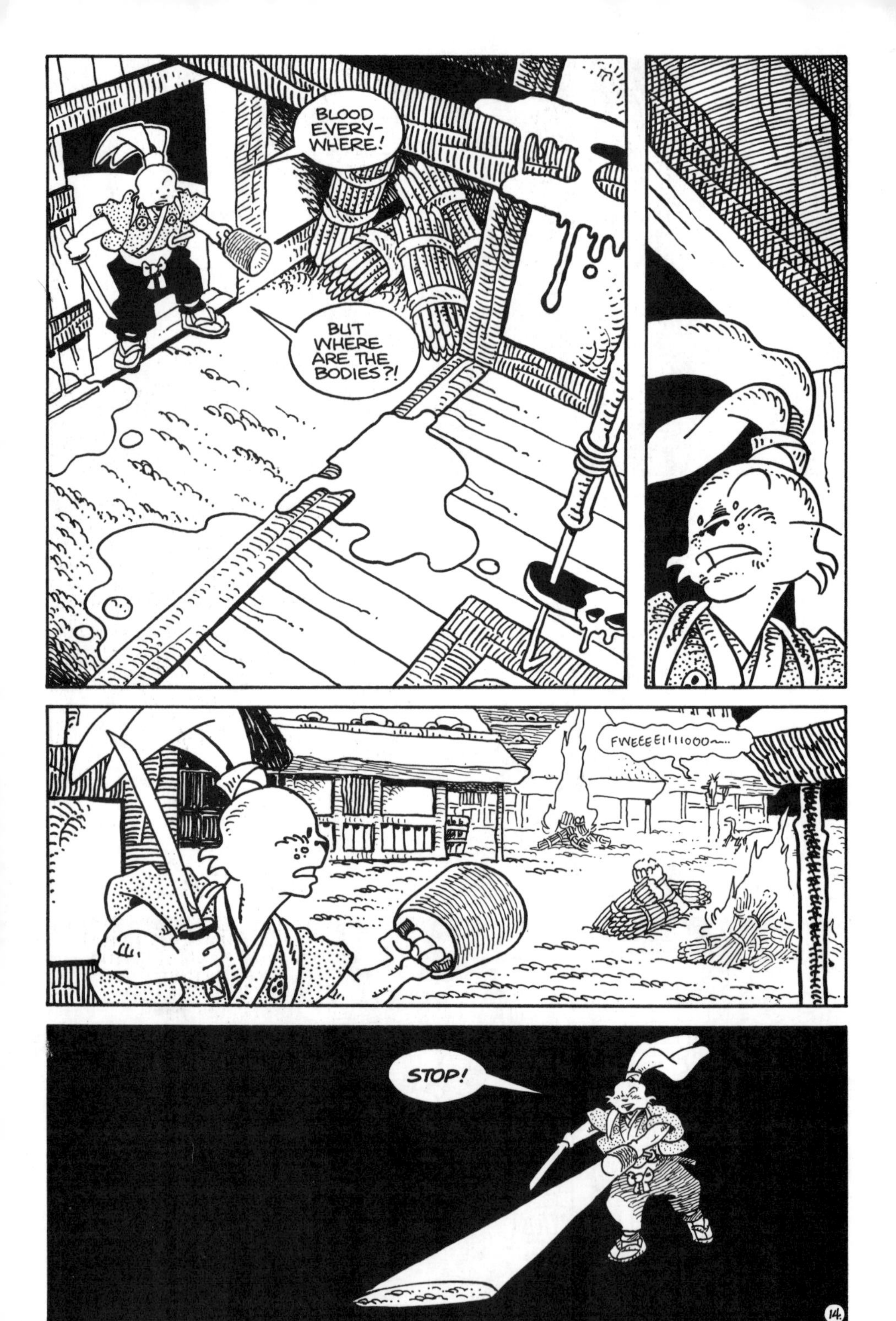
BLOOD EVERY-WHERE!
BUT WHERE ARE THE BODIES?!
FWEEEEIIIIOOO—...
STOP!
14.

HE'S DISAPPEARED-- ALONG WITH THE MUSIC!

WHA--?
THE GREEN ONE!

THE STRAINS ARE GROWING--
--COMING FROM THIS WAY!

IT'S GETTING DARKER AGAIN! I CAN BARELY SEE THE FULL MOON!

WHAT'S THAT?

¡GASP!¡

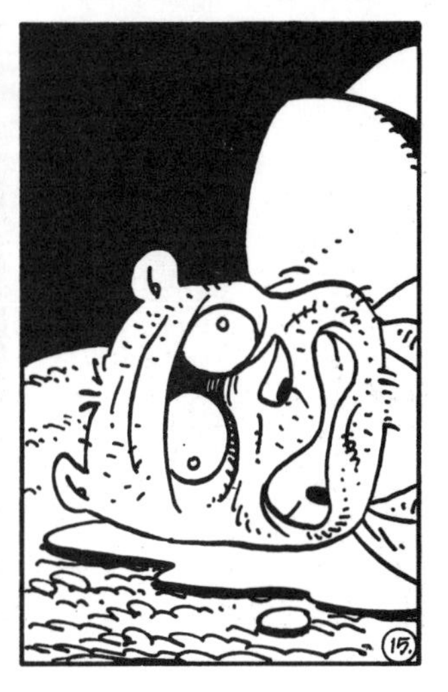
15.

THE MUSIC IS COMING FROM THIS WAY NOW!
THE BLACKNESS IS ALMOST TOTAL.

MOOOAAANN...
EYAHH!

WHO ARE YOU? WHO ARE YOU?!
THE HEAD MAN WAS MY HUSBAND!
THAT FLUTE-PLAYING FIEND HAS KILLED HIM!
SOB! SOB!

THE FLUTE MUSIC IS COMING FROM OVER THERE.
HELP ME, SAMURAI, HELP ME!
GO TO A NEIGHBOR'S HOME AND SECURE THE DOOR!
HEH HEH HEH HEH!

WHAT DID YOU SAY?
16

EEYAAHHHHH
HANYA*!
*FEMALE DEMON

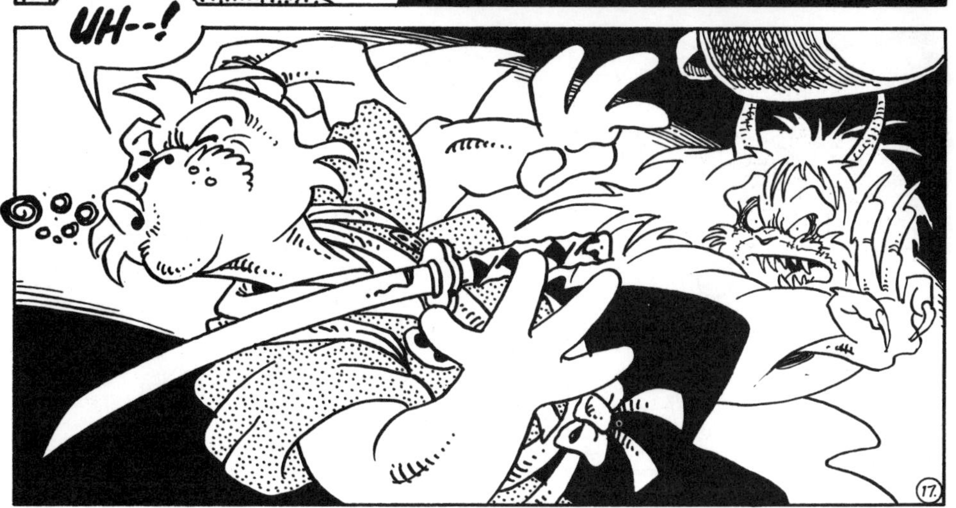
UH--!
17.

HEH HEH HEH!
RUNNING IS FUTILE, SAMURAI!

FOOOOOMM!

MAYBE FIRE WILL DESTROY YOU, WITCH!
FLOOSH!
18

GHAA! YOU'LL SUFFER FOR THIS, SAMURAI!
HYAAAH!

DO YOU THINK MERE STEEL CAN DESTROY ME?!

MAYBE NOT, BUT I KNOW YOU CLOAK YOURSELF IN DARKNESS, SO LIGHT MUST WEAKEN YOU!

STAY BACK, HELL-SPAWN!
HEH HEH HEH! FOOLISH MORTAL-- TO THINK THAT LIGHT CAN DIMINISH MY POWERS!
I HAVE MUCH MORE AT MY COMMAND THAN YOU CAN IMAGINE!
19.

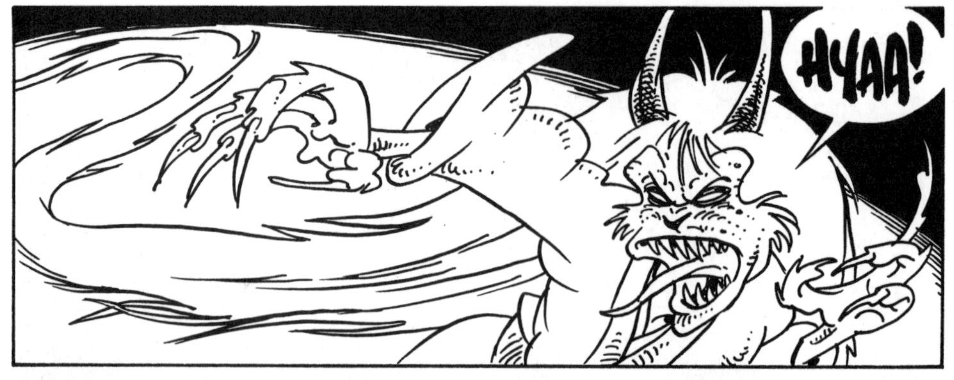
HYAA!

ULP!

HAHAHEEE--!!
ARHH!
20.

CURSE YOU, YOU FLUTE-PLAYING MONSTER!
HA HA HA!
YOU'LL DIE WITHOUT KNOWING THE TRUTH, SAMURAI!

.....

NO--!
21.

NO! NO!

NO-AGYAAAAAAHHHHH
SHOONK!

......

AND SO IT ENDS AT LAST...
22

I WAS A POOR COUNTRY SAMURAI AND WED TO A WOMAN WHO HUNGERED FOR POWER AND WEALTH. SHE CAUGHT THE EYE OF A HIGH-RANKING SAMURAI OF OUR LORD'S COURT.

HER SOUL BECAME SO CORRUPTED THAT SHE, OVER TIME, WAS TRANSFORMED INTO A *HANYA*.

THIS *TOKAGÉ*, A LOYAL PET, PINED FOR ME AND SOON DIED OF LONELINESS. HE JOINED ME ON MY QUEST.

THIS FLUTE, THAT SHE PLAYED WHEN STILL A MORTAL, DREW ME TO HER AS I HUNTED. IT WAS HER LINK TO THE MORTAL WORLD AND THE ONLY THING THAT COULD TRULY SLAY HER.

THAT'S WHY SHE RETREATED FROM ME LAST NIGHT! SHE HEARD THE FLUTE AND KNEW YOU WERE NEAR.

THE SUN'S RISING.
NOW THAT SHE IS DEAD, WHAT WILL HAPPEN TO YOU?

DID YOU HEAR ME?
I SAID--

!

IS IT SAFE TO COME OUT NOW, SAMURAI?
ARE YOU ALL RIGHT?
WHAT HAPPENED, SAMURAI?
IS THE EVIL GONE?

THE END.

MOMO-USAGI-TARO
THAT WAS A DELICIOUS MEAL.
DID I SEE SOME KIBI DANGO* BACK THERE?
YOU SURE DID, SAMURAI. WE JUST MADE SOME THIS MORNING!
I'LL BRING ONE OUT AND YOU CAN HAVE IT WITH YOUR TEA.
I'LL BE RIGHT BACK!
ZZZ...
*MILLET CAKE

IT'S BEEN A WHILE SINCE I'VE HAD ONE OF THESE.

EH--?

1.

YOU LOOK LIKE YOU WANT THIS MORE THAN I DO.

OH WELL, HERE YOU ARE. ENJOY IT.
I HOPE IT'S OKAY WITH YOUR PARENTS.

MUNCH! MUNCH! SCARF!
INNKEEPER-- ANOTHER KIBI DANGO PLEASE...
...IF YOU STILL HAVE ONE.
YAWN!
OH, YES, SAMURAI. WE'VE GOT PLENTY!

THANK YOU.
PLEASE ENJOY IT, SAMURAI.

SCARF! MUNCH! SMACK!

SO...IS THIS YOUR SISTER? ARE YOU GOING TO SHARE WITH HER?
NO, HUH?

I GUESS I CAN AFFORD TO BE GENEROUS. AFTER ALL, I'M GOING TO CLAIM GEN'S REWARD. HE WON'T MIND TREATING A KID TO SOME SWEETS. BESIDES, IT WOULD BE CRUEL TO GIVE HIM A TREAT AND NOT HER.
INNKEEPER-- ANOTHER *KIBI DANGO!*
RIGHT AWAY!

BUT...
WHERE DID **YOU** COME FROM?!

SIGH! IT LOOKS LIKE I'LL HAVE TO BE EVEN MORE GENEROUS THAN I INTENDED!
OH, INN-KEEPER--!

SOON...
YOU CAN'T ALL BE RELATED!
WHERE ARE YOU FROM?!

AH, THERE YOU ARE, CHILDREN! I'M GLAD YOU WAITED FOR ME.
WHAT HAVE YOU GOT THERE?

KIBI DANGO? WHERE DID YOU ALL GET THE SWEETS?
UH... I SORT OF TREATED THEM. I...I HOPE IT WAS OKAY.
I AM MIYAMOTO USAGI.

WELL, THANK YOU, USAGI-SAN. IT'S NOT OFTEN THE CHILDREN HAVE TREATS. THEY'RE FROM AN ORPHANAGE, YOU KNOW. I'M THEIR MATRON.

WE'RE RETURNING FROM A TRIP TO THE COUNTRYSIDE. SOME OF THE FARMERS GIVE US THEIR OFF-GRADE VEGETABLE SURPLUS. PEOPLE ARE SO KIND, YOU KNOW. WE EVEN HAVE A PATRON WHO DROPS OFF DONATIONS THAT KEEP US GOING MONTH AFTER MONTH... SUCH A NICE GUY.
MIND IF I SIT DOWN AWHILE?

HE SAYS WE SHOULD ALL LOOK OUT FOR ONE ANOTHER. HE SAYS THAT, YOU KNOW. IT'S TRUE, ISN'T IT? WE SHOULD LOOK OUT FOR EACH OTHER. IN RETURN FOR YOUR GENEROSITY PERHAPS YOU'LL HAVE SUPPER WITH US AT THE ORPHANAGE. THE CHILDREN WILL BE DELIGHTED TO HAVE YOU AS OUR GUEST, YOU KNOW.
4.

WHAT'S THAT RACKET UP THE ROAD? WHERE ARE THE CHILDREN RUNNING OFF TO? THEY CAN GET INTO SO MUCH MISCHIEF, YOU KNOW!
I WAS LIKE THAT.

HIYA HIYA HIYA! WE ARE THE UNAGIYAMA ENTERTAINMENT TROUPE! WE'VE COME TO YOUR AREA TO AMAZE AND ASTOUND YOU!
HIYA HIYA HIYA!
DON! DON! DON!

YAYY! IT'S A SHOW! IT'S A SHOW! HOORAY!

THAT'S RIGHT, KIDS! WE'LL BE IN TOWN FOR ONLY TWO MONTHS! COME AND SEE US, HUH?
WE'VE GOT ACROBATS, KNIFE THROWERS, JUGGLERS, MUSICIANS, MAGICIANS, FAN DANCERS, PUPPETEERS, AND A NEW KIND OF SHOW CALLED KABUKI!
COME AND SEE US BEFORE IT'S TOO LATE!
5.

"KABUKI"?! WHAT'S THAT?
I'VE HEARD OF IT.
IT'S A STAGE PLAY FOUNDED JUST A FEW YEARS AGO BY A SHINTO PRIESTESS IN KYOTO.
SEE YOU IN TOWN, KIDS!
YAYYYYYYY
HAHAHA!
YOW!

THE ACTORS' MOVEMENTS ARE VERY STYLIZED AND EXAGGERATED. I--
YAYYY! CAN WE GO, HUH? CAN WE SEE THE SHOW?
CAN WE, HUH? CAN WE?

HOW ABOUT YOU, UNCLE USAGI? WILL YOU TAKE US?
NO, I'M AFRAID WE DON'T HAVE THE FUNDS TO SPEND ON SUCH ENTERTAINMENT!
CHILDREN! HOW RUDE!

NO, BUT I'LL TELL YOU A STORY AFTER SUPPER!
YOU WILL? WHAT STORY?

WELL...UH... HOW ABOUT MOMO-USAGI-TARO?
YAYY!! UNCLE USAGI'S GOING TO TELL US A STORY!
6.

HERE'S SOME TEA, USAGI-SAN. I HOPE YOU ENJOYED YOUR MEAL.

AHH, IT WAS DELICIOUS, THANK YOU. IT'S RARE THAT A RONIN* GETS TREATED AS SUCH AN HONORED GUEST!
OH, YOU FLATTERER, YOU!
HA HA!
*MASTERLESS SAMURAI

WHAT SHOULD WE DO NOW, CHILDREN?!
STORY! STORY! STORY!
STORY!
HA HA!
MOMO-USAGI-TARO!
HA HA! GO AHEAD, USAGI-SAN!
IT WILL GIVE ME TIME TO WASH UP, YOU KNOW.
YAY! UNCLE USAGI'S GOING TO TELL US A STORY!
STORY-TIME!
SHH--! QUIET!
BEGIN THE STORY, UNCLE USAGI! BEGIN THE STORY!
1.

MUKASHI, MUKASHI--A LONG, LONG TIME AGO--OJII-SAN AND OBAA-SAN LIVED A QUIET LIFE IN THE MOUNTAINS. THEY HAD NO CHILDREN, BUT EVEN AT THEIR AGE THEY PRAYED TO THE GODS FOR A LITTLE ONE OF THEIR OWN.

"OJII-SAN HAD BEEN A MIGHTY WARRIOR IN HIS YOUTH AND LIVED IN A HUGE CASTLE, BUT NOW WAS CONTENT WITH THE SIMPLE COUNTRY LIFE.

"AS OJII-SAN WAS UP IN THE MOUNTAINS GATHERING THE WEEK'S FIREWOOD, OBAA-SAN WENT TO THE FRIGID STREAM WHERE SHE WASHED THEIR CLOTHES. TO HER SURPRISE, THE WATER WAS STRANGELY WARM AND PLEASANT.

"OBAA-SAN PRETENDED THE CLOTHES SHE WASHED BELONGED TO THEIR SON, AND SHE SOFTLY HUMMED LULLABIES AS SHE WORKED.
EEP!
EH? WHAT IS IT? DO YOU SEE SOMETHING?

OYO--?! WHAT IS THAT FLOATING DOWN-STREAM?
COULD IT REALLY BE A GIANT PEACH?!
8

The water is bitter far away--
where great lords wash their feet.
The water is sweet over here--
leave the bitter and come to the sweet.

HA! WHAT GOOD FORTUNE! WE'LL SURELY HAVE A GREAT FEAST TONIGHT!

"SHE WAITED PATIENTLY FOR OJII-SAN'S RETURN. BUT AS THEY WERE ABOUT TO CUT THE LUSCIOUS FRUIT IN HALF...
!
RIIIPP!

A CHILD! A PERFECT BABY BOY!
GLBBLX.

THE GODS HAVE ANSWERED OUR PRAYERS!
WE WILL NAME HIM MOMO-USAGI-TARO-- PEACH-RABBIT-BOY!
BLXPIP! HA HA!
EEP!
9.

"FROM THAT MOMENT ON THEIR HOME ECHOED WITH THE SOUNDS OF JOY, AND YEARS PASSED QUICKLY.

HA HA HA!

"BUT ONE DAY...
FATHER, I AM TROUBLED.
WHAT IS IT, MOMO-USAGI-TARO?

I HAD A DREAM--THE MOST VIVID I HAVE EVER HAD. IN IT, EVIL ONI* CAME BY SEA TO PLUNDER AND DESTROY!
*OGRES

THEY WERE FIERCE IN THEIR BRUTALITY, AND MANY WERE LEFT WEEPING IN THEIR WAKE!
WHY DID I DREAM THIS, FATHER?

IT WAS NO DREAM BUT A VISION FROM THE GODS. I, MYSELF, FOUGHT THE ONI IN MY YOUTH! MANY YEARS HAVE PASSED SINCE THEY LEFT THEIR ISLAND FORTRESS, BUT I FEAR THEY WILL COME TO RAID AGAIN SOON.

ON MY HONOR, I SWEAR THAT NEVER AGAIN WILL THE ONI HURT THE INNOCENT! I WILL DEPART FOR THE INLAND SEA TOMORROW!
WELL SAID, MY SON!
11.

CAW!
CAW!
CAW!
CAW!
CAW!
CAW!

I WILL SOON BE READY TO FACE THE *ONI'S* MENACE.
WE HAVE GIFTS TO HELP YOU IN YOUR QUEST.
POUND
POUND

I GIVE TO YOU THE SWORD I RAISED IN BATTLE WHEN WE FIRST DROVE THE *ONI* INVADERS FROM OUR LAND.
I WILL WEAR IT WITH HONOR, AS YOU DID, FATHER.

AND FOR YOUR JOURNEY, *NIPPON ICHI NO KIBI DANGO*-- THE BEST MILLET CAKES IN THE LAND -- MADE BY OUR OWN HANDS.
A WARRIOR'S FOOD! IT WILL SUSTAIN ME DURING MY QUEST.

GOOD-BYE, MY SON! YOU BRING HONOR TO OUR FAMILY!
COME BACK SAFELY!
EEP!
12.

CHIP!
CHIRP!
MOO!

I HAVE TRAVELED FAR TODAY. I'M FAMISHED.
I WILL ENJOY MY MEAL.

GRRR...

DO YOU KNOW WHOM YOU GROWL AT, BEAST?!
I AM INU, THE LORD OF THE FOREST FLOOR! YOU MUST BE MOMO-USAGI-TARO!
ALL IN THE FOREST KNOW OF YOUR JOURNEY TO BATTLE THE ONI!
WHAT DO YOU WANT?

IS THAT NIPPON ICHI NO KIBI DANGO IN YOUR POUCH?
GIVE ME ONE, AND I WILL JOIN YOU!

WHY WOULD I NEED YOUR HELP?
I WILL SHOW YOU!

INDEED, YOUR STRENGTH IS IMPRESSIVE!
CRAKK!
日本一

I WOULD WELCOME YOUR COMPANIONSHIP AFTER ALL. I WILL NOT GIVE YOU A WHOLE KIBI DANGO, BUT I WILL SHARE ONE WITH YOU.
VERY WELL.

"AND SO...
14.

"THE NEXT DAY...

HO HO HO HO HO!

!
HO HO HO!

HO HO!
GROWL!

GRRRR--! COME DOWN HERE! I'LL TEAR YOU APART!
HO HO HO!

LEAVE HIM ALONE, INU-SAN! WE MUST BE ON OUR WAY!
WAIT!
15

I JUST WANTED TO SEE IF YOU ARE REALLY MOMO-USAGI-TARO! I AM **SARU,** LORD OF THE TREES!

IS THAT *NIPPON ICHI NO KIBI DANGO* YOU CARRY? GIVE ME ONE, AND I WILL JOIN YOU!

WE COULD USE SOMEONE AS CLEVER AS YOU. I WILL NOT GIVE YOU A WHOLE *KIBI DANGO,* BUT I WILL SHARE ONE WITH YOU.

"THE NEXT DAY THE FRIENDS REACHED A GRASSY PLAIN...
NO *ONI* CAN MATCH MY STRENGTH!
...OR MY AGILITY!

DON'T GET OVERCONFIDENT! AFTER ALL, THERE ARE ONLY THREE OF US AGAINST AN ENTIRE ISLAND!
K
EH--?

Killlllll...
HO! IT'S JUST A BIRD!
GRR... LET'S IGNORE IT AND CONTINUE ON.
日本一
16.

KI
EYOW!
YIKE!

YOU ARE A BRAVE BIRD!
I AM KIJI, LORD OF THE SKIES!
MOMO-USAGI-TARO--IS THAT NIPPON ICHI NO KIBI DANGO YOU CARRY?

GIVE ME ONE, AND I WILL FOLLOW YOU!
I CANNOT GIVE YOU A WHOLE KIBI DANGO, BUT I WILL SHARE ONE WITH YOU.

"THEY SOON REACHED THE INLAND SEA WHERE THEY BOARDED A WAITING SHIP.
17.

"THE CROSSING TOOK MANY DAYS OVER STORM-TOSSED WATERS UNTIL...
SUCH A FEARSOME-LOOKING ISLAND! THAT MUST SURELY BE THE STRONGHOLD OF THE *ONI*!

"BUT THE TERRIBLE RESIDENTS WERE NOT TAKEN UNAWARES...
LOOK! I SEE A GIANT PEACH!
A SAIL!
WE ARE BEING ATTACKED!
BACK TO THE CASTLE! WE MUST WARN THE KING!

"SO WHEN THE HEROES REACHED THE ISLAND...
HO! THEY THINK THEY ARE SAFE, LOCKED WITHIN THEIR FORTRESS!
KIIIIIIII...
THEY MUST HAVE THOUGHT WE WERE A HUGE INVASION PARTY!
I CAN FLY OVER THE CASTLE WALLS AND ATTACK THEM FROM ABOVE!
EVEN WALLS WILL NOT STOP US!
18.

KI!!!!!!!!!!!!!
YAHH!

HO HO HO!

KI!!!!!!!
KEEP THEM BUSY, FRIEND KIJI...

...AND I WILL LET OUR COMRADES IN!

HIYAAHH!
HO HO HO!
RRRROWLL!!
19.

"THE BATTLE LASTED A FULL DAY AND NIGHT...

"WHEN THE SUN ROSE, MOMO-USAGI-TARO FOUND HIMSELF FACE TO FACE WITH THE ONI KING!

GRAHH!!
CHOK!

20.

RYAAAAHG!!
EYAAAH!
CHOP!
CHOP!

EYAH YAHH YAHH! WITHOUT MY HORNS I AM POWERLESS!

MERCY, WARRIOR, MERCY! I VOW TO REPENT AND MAKE RESTITUTION!
HOW?

"THE ONI KING REVEALED THE VAST TREASURE PLUNDERED OVER THE YEARS-- GOLD, CORAL, TORTOISE SHELL, JADE, SWORDS, AND MUCH MORE.
ALL THIS I GIVE TO YOU WITH MY PLEDGE NEVER TO PILLAGE AGAIN!
VERY WELL.
21.

"MOMO-USAGI-TARO RETURNED THE WEALTH TO THOSE IT WAS STOLEN FROM BUT THERE WAS STILL MUCH LEFT OVER."

WITH IT HE BUILT A HUGE CASTLE WHERE HIS BELOVED PARENTS LIVED OUT THEIR DAYS, AND HE AND HIS COMPANIONS CONTINUED TO DO MANY GOOD AND HEROIC DEEDS.

WELL, THEY'RE FAST ASLEEP. I DON'T KNOW IF THAT'S A COMPLIMENT OR AN INSULT TO MY STORYTELLING ABILITIES.
HA HA! IT *IS* WELL PAST THEIR BEDTIME, YOU KNOW.
WILL YOU HELP ME TUCK THEM IN?
OF COURSE.

LATER...
WELL, I'LL BE ON MY WAY NOW. THANK YOU FOR YOUR HOSPITALITY.
AND THANK YOU FOR YOUR GENEROSITY, USAGI-SAN.

GOOD-BYE, USAGI-SAN. PLEASE STOP BY WHEN YOU ARE IN THIS AREA AGAIN.
22

I WAS OUT ALL DAY TODAY. TOMORROW WILL BE AN ESPECIALLY BUSY DAY.

MY, THE STARS LOOK PARTICULARLY BEAUTIFUL TONIGHT.

ADMIRING THE NIGHT SKY, MATRON?
EH?

IT'S RARE THAT YOU TAKE EVEN A FEW MINUTES FOR YOURSELF.
YOU REALLY SHOULD DO IT MORE OFTEN.
AH, INUKAI-SAN! IT IS ALWAYS GOOD TO SEE YOU!
I WAS SAYING GOOD-BYE TO A FRIEND.
A NICE SAMURAI HELPED US. HE ENTERTAINED THE CHILDREN WHILE I GOT SOME WORK DONE. HE EVEN HELPED PUT THEM TO BED, YOU KNOW.
A SAMURAI, YOU SAY? THAT WAS KIND OF HIM.

IT'S TOO BAD I MISSED HIM. I WOULD LIKE TO MEET A SAMURAI WHO'S GOOD FOR SOMETHING!
HA HA! OH, YOU--! I'M SURE YOU TWO WOULD HAVE BEEN GOOD FRIENDS.

WELL, MAYBE SOMEDAY--IF THE GODS WILL IT--WE WILL MEET.
NOW IT'S TIME YOU TURNED IN YOURSELF. YOU WORK MUCH TOO HARD.
YOU'RE RIGHT. THIS HAS BEEN A LONG DAY.
23.

OH, THIS GOLD SHOULD KEEP THIS PLACE RUNNING FOR A FEW MORE MONTHS.
YOU'RE TOO GENEROUS, INUKAI-SAN. WHAT WOULD THIS ORPHANAGE DO WITHOUT YOU?
WELL, IN THIS WORLD WE ALL HAVE TO LOOK OUT FOR EACH OTHER.
YES. I'VE OFTEN HEARD YOU SAY THAT.
I NOTICED AN ENTERTAINMENT TROUPE IN TOWN. MAYBE THERE'S ENOUGH TO TAKE THE CHILDREN TO SEE A SHOW.
YES, I'M CERTAIN WE'LL BE ABLE TO MANAGE THAT NOW.

"I'M SURE THE CHILDREN WILL ENJOY IT, INUKAI-SAN. NOW COME IN, AND I WILL FIX YOU SOMETHING TO EAT."

OH--!

I'M SORRY I STARTLED YOU. ARE YOU OKAY?
ER...YES... EX--EXCUSE ME, SAMURAI.

WHAT A BEAUTIFUL GIRL.
SHE SEEMS TO BE IN A BIG HURRY.
I WONDER WHAT'S WRONG.
STOP IT, USAGI! YOU'RE READING TOO MUCH INTO HER ACTIONS!
BESIDES, IT'S NOT YOUR CONCERN.
SHE PROBABLY JUST WANTS TO GET HOME TO HER FAMILY.

THE END.

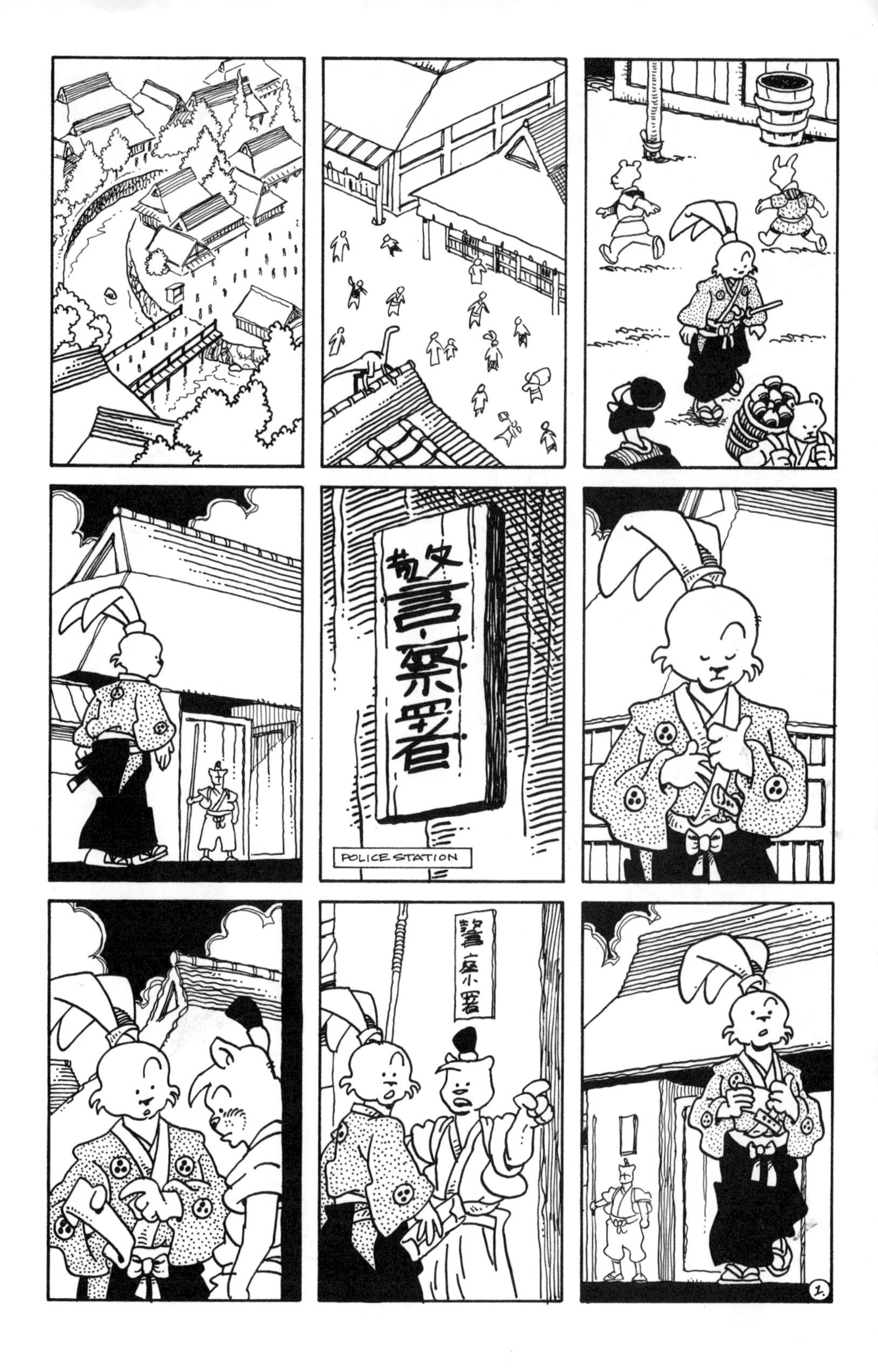
POLICE STATION
1.

The Case of the
HAIR PIN MURDERS
AN INSPECTOR ISHIDA MYSTERY!
TURNIPS! I'VE GOT TURNIPS FOR SALE!
HOI HOI HOI! COME IN AND SEE THE UNAGIYAMA ENTERTAINMENT TROUPE! KNIFE THROWERS! MAGICIANS! ACROBATS! MUSICIANS!
THAT GIRL-- SHE'S THE ONE I SAW LAST NIGHT.
THE WAY SHE LOOKS OVER HER SHOULDER--SHE'S AFRAID!
IT-- IT'S PROBABLY JUST MY IMAGINATION...
...AND CERTAINLY NO CONCERN OF MINE.
2.

A BEAUTIFUL PRINCESS SAVES THE COUNTRY FROM A MAD MONK WHO CAPTURES THE RAIN! COME AND SEE THE *KABUKI* PLAY ***NARUKAMI THE THUNDER GOD!***
HOI HOI HOI!
WELCOME. PLEASE ENJOY THE SHOW.

THIS IS THE PLACE THAT THE GUARD SAID I SHOULD FIND HIM.
I WONDER WHY THERE'S A CROWD.
3.

EXCUSE ME. STEP ASIDE, PLEASE.

EXCUSE ME. I HAVE BUSINESS WITH SOMEONE HERE.

WHAT?!

WHEN ARE THE BODY REMOVERS GETTING HERE?
THEY'VE BEEN SUMMONED, SIR.
WHAT'S GOING ON?
IF YOU MUST KNOW, HE WAS JUST FOUND DEAD IN THIS ALLEY, SAMURAI!
YOU THERE-- KEEP BACK!

THE WAY I SEE IT, HIS HEART GAVE OUT, HE GRABBED THE BARREL FOR SUPPORT, AND THEN HE DIED.
THERE IS NO FOUL PLAY AT WORK HERE!

NOT TRUE.
EH?
4.

THERE IS A SMALL WOUND ON THE BACK OF HIS NECK. YOU CAN SEE A SPOT OF DRIED BLOOD THERE.
WHAT?

ARE YOU TRYING TO TELL ME MY JOB?! I OUGHT TO ARREST YOU FOR INTERFERING!
IS ANYTHING THE MATTER?

:GULP!: INSPECTOR...AH... I'M...ER...DEALING WITH A TROUBLEMAKER, SIR!
I WAS JUST MAKING AN OBSERVATION.
QUIET, YOU!
WHAT SORT OF OBSERVATION?
THERE'S NOTHING TO SEE HERE!
EVERY-BODY, GO HOME!

BUT SURELY, SIR, HE'S JUST RIFFRAFF...
EVEN RIFF-RAFF HAVE EYES, JUNIOR INSPECTOR NII!
NOW, SAMURAI, WHAT DID YOU SEE?

A SMALL PUNCTURE ON THE NECK. YOU CAN SEE A SLIGHT DISCOLORATION AROUND THE WOUND.
HMM...
A SHARP NEEDLE SLIPPED BETWEEN THE VERTEBRAE CAN CAUSE INSTANT DEATH.
5.

THERE'S ALSO A TRACE OF WHITE POWDER ON HIS SHOULDER.
SO THERE IS.

RICE FLOUR-- THE SORT THAT WOMEN USE FOR MAKE-UP.
YOU HAVE KEEN POWERS OF OBSERVATION, SAMURAI.

DO YOU KNOW WHO THE VICTIM IS, OFFICER NII?
HE WAS TENDO MASAYUKI, A PROMINENT SILK MERCHANT.

SO, WE KNOW WHO THE VICTIM IS...
...BUT WHO ARE **YOU**, SAMURAI? I DO NOT RECOGNIZE YOU AS FROM THIS TOWN.

I AM MIYAMOTO USAGI. I AM LOOKING FOR INSPECTOR ISHIDA. I WAS TOLD THAT I COULD FIND HIM HERE.
AND YOU HAVE. I AM ISHIDA. WHAT CAN I DO FOR YOU, USAGI-SAN?

I WAS REFERRED BY PRIEST SANSHOBO. HE SAID YOU ARE AN HONORABLE PERSON AND MIGHT BE ABLE TO HELP ME.
I HAVE HIGH REGARD FOR THE PRIEST. WHAT SERVICE CAN I RENDER?
THE BODY REMOVERS ARE HERE.
6.

I WOULD LIKE TO CLAIM THE BOUNTY FOR HOSOKU THE BANDIT. HERE IS THE RECEIPT FOR HIS CAPTURE.
I WOULD NOT HAVE TAKEN YOU FOR A BOUNTY HUNTER.

I'M COLLECTING IT FOR A FRIEND WHO IS STAYING AT PRIEST SANSHOBO'S TEMPLE.
IT SEEMS TO BE IN ORDER.

IT WILL BE A FEW DAYS BEFORE YOU RECEIVE YOUR MONEY.
OF COURSE. THANK YOU.
I'LL TAKE YOU TO THE STATION AND FILE YOUR REQUEST.

INSPECTOR ISHIDA!
EH? WHAT IS IT?

ANOTHER DEATH--AT THE HOME OF ABE THE SAKE BROKER!

USAGI-SAN, I HAVE TO INVESTIGATE THIS NEW CRIME SCENE BEFORE RETURNING TO THE STATION. YOU LOOK LIKE YOU'VE SEEN DEATH BEFORE. YOU CAN ACCOMPANY ME IF YOU LIKE.
THANK YOU, I WILL.
7.

THE HOME OF MERCHANT ABÉ...
IT LOOKS LIKE THIS ONE PUT UP A STRUGGLE.
HAS ANYTHING BEEN MOVED?
WE HAVE TOUCHED NOTHING, INSPECTOR ISHIDA.
WHO FOUND THE BODY?
THE HOUSEKEEPER, SIR. I WILL SUMMON HER.

HE HAS SOME RICE POWDER ON HIS SLEEVE.
TURN HIM OVER.

A BROKEN NEEDLE PROTRUDING FROM HIS NECK.
HERE'S THE REST OF IT!

A HAIRPIN! A WOMAN'S HAIRPIN!
8.

TWO IDENTICAL MURDERS...
WHAT?!
NO, THREE.

A LUMBER BROKER, BANCHO, WAS FOUND DEAD IN HIS OFFICE EARLY THIS MORNING. I HAD COME FROM THAT CRIME SCENE TO THE ALLEY WHERE I MET YOU.
THEY WERE ALL KILLED THE SAME WAY?
IT SEEMS TO BE THE CASE.

THEN YOU KNEW ABOUT THE NECK WOUND BACK IN THE ALLEY.
OF COURSE.
THEN WHY DID YOU LET ME ACCOMPANY YOU HERE?
I WANTED TO SEE HOW MUCH YOU KNEW--PERHAPS YOU ARE INVOLVED IN THE MURDERS.
BUT I THINK NOW THAT YOU ARE NOT.

BUT YOU ARE A SHARP OBSERVER, AND I COULD USE ALL THE HELP I CAN GET. OUR CULTURE, WITH ITS RELUCTANCE TO EXAMINE OR HANDLE THE DEAD, HAMPERS US. MANY MURDERS--FOR INSTANCE, BY POISONING--ARE OFTEN ATTRIBUTED TO NATURAL CAUSES BY A NEGLIGENT INVESTIGATOR.

I HAVE HEARD THAT FOREIGN DOCTORS TREAT THE EXAMINATION OF THE DEAD AS A SCIENCE--AN AUTOPSY, THEY CALL IT. SUCH PROCEDURES ARE ILLEGAL IN OUR COUNTRY. WE ARE RESTRICTED TO A MERE CURSORY LOOK.

WHICH SHOULD BE ENOUGH FOR ANY COMPETENT INVESTIGATOR!
EH--?
9.

THREE PROMINENT MERCHANTS WERE MURDERED LAST NIGHT!
SENIOR INSPECTOR OGAWA! WHAT A PLEASANT SURPRISE! I USUALLY DON'T SEE YOU SO EARLY IN THE MORNING!
DON'T BE A FOOL, ISHIDA! WHAT HAVE YOU LEARNED?

WE KNOW VERY LITTLE SO FAR, BUT THERE MUST BE SOME CONNECTION BETWEEN THE VICTIMS.

THINGS ARE NOT PROGRESSING! I THINK I SHOULD TAKE OVER THIS CASE.
NONSENSE. I WAS ON CALL WHEN THE REPORTS CAME IN. I REFUSE TO GIVE UP THIS CASE!

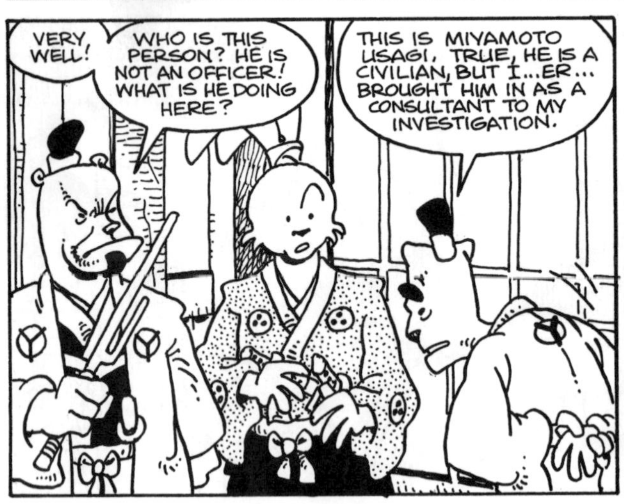
VERY WELL!
WHO IS THIS PERSON? HE IS NOT AN OFFICER! WHAT IS HE DOING HERE?
THIS IS MIYAMOTO USAGI. TRUE, HE IS A CIVILIAN, BUT I...ER... BROUGHT HIM IN AS A CONSULTANT TO MY INVESTIGATION.

HMM... MOST UNUSUAL. I WILL HAVE TO LOOK INTO THIS. IF THERE IS ANY IRREGULARITY, I WILL SEE TO YOUR DISMISSAL!
OF COURSE.
10.

WATCH YOUR STEP, ISHIDA!
I ALWAYS DO, CHIEF INSPECTOR.
ONE NEVER KNOWS WHAT ONE COULD STEP IN.
YOUR SUPERIOR?

YES. PLEASE FORGIVE US. OUR CONDUCT IN FRONT OF A STRANGER WAS INAPPROPRIATE.
ER... THINK NOTHING OF IT, INSPECTOR ISHIDA.
YOU ARE MOST GRACIOUS.

I AM SURPRISED THAT THE CHIEF INSPECTOR SHOWED UP HERE. HE USUALLY HAS NO INTEREST IN CASES BUT CONTENTS HIMSELF WITH CURRYING THE FAVORS OF THOSE INFLUENTIAL IN THE AREA. WHERE HE GETS THE FUNDS TO DO SO I DON'T KNOW.
WHY DID HE WANT TO TAKE OVER THIS CASE?

THESE ARE PROMINENT MERCHANTS. NO DOUBT HE WANTS THE ACCOLADES FOR FINDING THEIR KILLER.
IS HE A COMPETENT INVESTIGATOR?

THERE ARE TALES THAT OGAWA RECEIVED HIS POSITION THROUGH BRIBERY, NOT ABILITY... FORGIVE ME. HE IS MY SUPERIOR, AND I HAVE ALREADY SPOKEN TOO MUCH.
I HOPE MY PRESENCE HERE DOES NOT GET YOU INTO TROUBLE.
DON'T GIVE IT A SECOND THOUGHT.
11.

INSPECTOR ISHIDA, THIS IS THE HOUSEKEEPER. SHE REPORTED THE CRIME.
I HAVE BEEN WITH MASTER ABÉ SINCE HE SET UP HIS BUSINESS.
DO YOU KNOW WHO KILLED HIM?

WELL, YOU SEE... HE WAS WITH A WOMAN LAST NIGHT. AT TIMES I TRY TO BE DISCREET AND WITHDRAW EARLY.

I DON'T KNOW WHO SHE WAS, BUT SHE WAS VERY BEAUTIFUL. SHE COULD HAVE BEEN A YUJO* FROM THE LOTUS HOUSE.
*COURTESAN

YOU DON'T THINK SHE KILLED HIM, DO YOU?
WE DON'T KNOW. GO ON.
WELL, WHEN I CAME IN TO SERVE HIM HIS BREAKFAST, I FOUND HIM AS YOU SEE HIM NOW.

ER... WHAT IS HIS CONNECTION WITH MERCHANTS BANCHO AND TENDO?

WHY, I BELIEVE ALL THREE WERE APPRENTICED TO MERCHANT HAYATE, WHO WAS MURDERED... OH, ABOUT FIFTEEN OR SO YEARS AGO.
12.

ACCORDING TO THE HOUSEKEEPER, MERCHANT HAYATE LIVED ON THE SOUTH SIDE OF TOWN.
WHY ARE THESE PEOPLE RUNNING?

IS THERE TROUBLE?
TWO SAMURAI ARE TEARING UP THE MARKETPLACE!

THIS IS ***MY*** BUSINESS, USAGI! LET ME HANDLE IT!
AS YOU WISH.

HAW HAW HAW!
GLUG! GLUG!
ER... IF I CAN BE OF HELP...
THANK YOU, USAGI. I WILL CALL ON YOU.
13

PARDON ME. YOU ARE UNDER ARREST FOR DISTURBING THE PEACE. PLEASE COME QUIETLY. I DON'T WANT TO HURT YOU
WHAT?!
NGGHH!
BWAH! HA HA! I LIKE YOUR SPUNK, OLD MAN--
--BUT IT WON'T SAVE YOU!

YOU ARROGANT COP!
AGGHH!
HA HA! LEAVE SOME OF HIM FOR ME! GLUG! GLUG! AHHH!

I'M COMING, ISHIDA!

PLEASE HEED MY WARNING.
I'LL TEAR YOUR EARS OFF!

HHIYAHHH!
THOK!
OOGH!
14

GYAHH!
THUD!

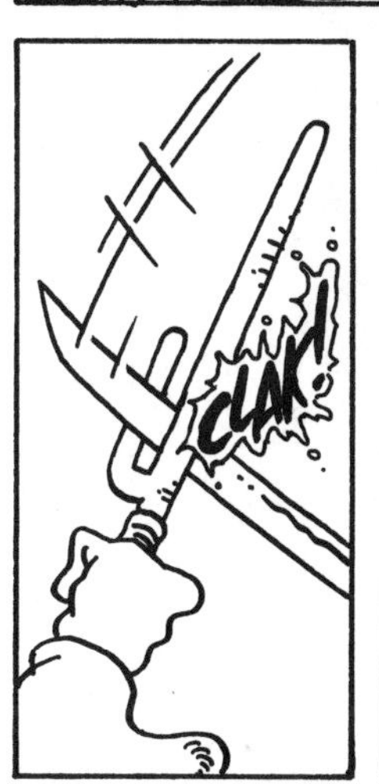
CLAK!

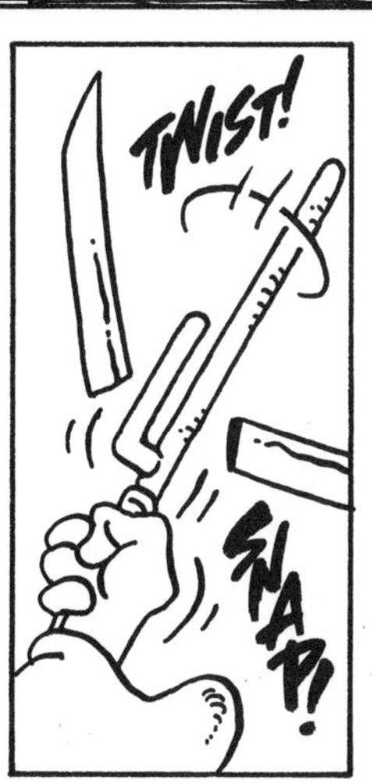
TWIST!
SNAP!

YAHH!
UH--!

TWIZZ!

UH... GOOD WORK.
THANK YOU.
IT WAS NOTHING.
LIKE MOST BIG BULLIES, THEY ARE UNSKILLED AS FIGHTERS.
15

LATER...
HMM... THIS LOOKS LIKE THE AREA THAT MERCHANT HAYATE HAD HIS SHOP.

EXCUSE ME. WE ARE LOOKING INTO A CRIME THAT TOOK PLACE AROUND HERE FIFTEEN YEARS AGO.
FIFTEEN YEARS AGO, YOU SAY? MY, THAT'S A LONG TIME!

MY FATHER-IN-LAW MAY BE ABLE TO HELP YOU, SIRS. HE HAS BEEN HERE FOR THIRTY YEARS.
THANK YOU.

MERCHANT HAYATE, HUH? HMM... YES, I KNEW HIM VERY WELL... SUCH A TRAGEDY.
TELL US ABOUT IT.

HMM...YES...WELL, HAYATE WAS A FABRIC BROKER. HE AND HIS WIFE WERE MURDERED, AND THEIR DAUGHTER AND SON WERE GIVEN TO RELATIVES WHO OWN AN INN IN THE NEXT PROVINCE.
16.

HOW OLD WERE THE CHILDREN?
HMM... LET ME SEE... THE DAUGHTER WAS ABOUT... HMM... THIRTEEN AND THE SON ABOUT SEVEN.

CAN YOU TELL ME THE DETAILS OF THE MURDERS?
HMM... LET ME REMEMBER... HAYATE HAD JUST SOLD A HUGE CONSIGNMENT OF DRY GOODS TO LORD YAMAHASHI. ALL THE MONEY HAD DISAPPEARED, SO IT WAS THOUGHT ROBBERY WAS THE MOTIVE.

AT FIRST, PEOPLE SUSPECTED HIS THREE APPRENTICES... BUT THEY ALL HAD SOLID ALIBIS.
HOWEVER, THERE WAS A SAMURAI... HMM... NATTO WAS HIS NAME... WHO WAS A FRIEND OF THEIRS.
IT WAS THOUGHT THAT **HE** DID THE ACTUAL KILLINGS, BUT NOTHING WAS EVER PROVEN.

I HEARD THE THREE APPRENTICES SET UP THEIR OWN BUSINESSES AND ARE DOING WELL.
HMM... NO ONE KNOWS WHAT BECAME OF THAT SAMURAI.

THAT IS ALL I CAN RECALL. I HOPE I HAVE BEEN OF SERVICE.
YOU HAVE, THANK YOU.
17.

SO... THE DAUGHTER SEEMS TO BE THE PRIME SUSPECT.
BUT WILL THE KILLINGS END WITH THE MURDER OF THE THREE MERCHANTS?

YOU MEAN THAT SAMURAI-- *NATTO?* DO YOU THINK SHE WOULD ATTEMPT TO SLAY EVEN A *SAMURAI?*
SHE WAITED FIFTEEN YEARS FOR HER REVENGE. I THINK SHE'LL TRY ANYTHING.

YES. I FEAR YOU ARE RIGHT.

THEN WE WILL HAVE TO FIND NATTO. WE CAN CHECK WITH THE LOCAL LORD. PERHAPS NATTO IS IN HIS SERVICE.

AND IF HE HAS LEFT THE AREA?
I FEAR THERE IS VERY LITTLE I CAN DO.
18.

I AM INSPECTOR ISHIDA. I REQUEST AN AUDIENCE WITH CHAMBERLAIN TOYOFUKU REGARDING A CURRENT INVESTIGATION.
OUR LORD YAMAHASHI IS ILL, AND THE CHAMBERLAIN HAS ASSUMED MANY OF HIS DUTIES. BUT I WILL SEE IF HE IS AVAILABLE.

I CAN ONLY AFFORD YOU A FEW MINUTES.
WHAT INFORMATION CAN I GIVE YOU?

CHAMBERLAIN TOYOFUKU, THANK YOU FOR YOUR PRECIOUS TIME.
THREE MERCHANTS HAVE BEEN MURDERED, AND EVIDENCE SUGGESTS THAT A SAMURAI MAY BE THE NEXT VICTIM. WE NEED YOUR PERMISSION TO EXAMINE THE CLAN ARCHIVES TO DETERMINE HIS CURRENT WHEREABOUTS.

"ARCHIVES"? **BAH!** WHY DO YOU BOTHER ME WITH DETAILS? VERY WELL. WHO IS THIS SAMURAI?

WE KNOW HIM ONLY AS ***NATTO!***

"NATTO"?!
19

YOU KNOW HIM?
Y-YES...
I-I MEAN **NO!**

I MEAN I KNOW **OF** HIM. HE WAS EXCUSED FROM OUR LORD'S SERVICE MANY YEARS AGO.
HE HAS SINCE LEFT THE AREA.

BUT IF I CAN LOOK OVER THE RECORDS, PERHAPS I WILL FIND A CLUE TO WHERE HE IS AT PRESENT.
REQUEST **DENIED!**

THE OFFICIAL RECORDS CONTAIN CONFIDENTIAL INFORMATION.
SIR--IF DISCRETION IS AN ISSUE, I ASSURE YOU...
I SAID **NO!**

LORD YAMAHASHI CANNOT BE ASSOCIATED, EVEN REMOTELY, WITH A CRIMINAL INVESTIGATION!
THIS AUDIENCE IS ENDED!
20.

LATER, AT POLICE HEADQUARTERS...
YOU ARE NEW IN TOWN, USAGI. WHERE ARE YOU STAYING TONIGHT?
WELL, I HAVEN'T FOUND A ROOM AT AN INN YET...
GOOD. YOU'LL SPEND THE NIGHT IN MY HOME.
YOU'RE TOO GENEROUS.

SLAM!
ISHIDA!
INSPECTOR OGAWA!

I RECEIVED A COMPLAINT FROM CHAMBERLAIN TOYOFUKU'S OFFICE! HOW DARE YOU LINK LORD YAMAHASHI WITH A MURDER INVESTIGATION?!
IT WAS A LEGITIMATE INQUIRY! THE CHAMBERLAIN IS BEING UNREASONABLE!
NONSENSE!
WATCH YOUR WORDS, ISHIDA! "A CRITICISM OF A LORD'S RETAINER IS A CRITICISM OF THE LORD HIMSELF!"

NO ONE CAN BE PLACED ABOVE THE LAW! IT IS JUSTICE FOR ALL OR FOR NONE!
FOOL! DO YOU REALLY BELIEVE THAT?!

YES.
21.

DO NOT DISTURB CHAMBERLAIN TOYOFUKU AGAIN! UNDERSTAND?
YES, SENIOR INSPECTOR. I UNDERSTAND.
WHAT STEPS HAVE YOU TAKEN TO FIND THE KILLER?

WE SUSPECT THE MURDERER TO BE A WOMAN--THE DAUGHTER OF A MERCHANT HAYATE, WHO, HIMSELF, WAS MURDERED FIFTEEN YEARS AGO.

I SENT OFFICER NII TO AN INN IN THE NEIGHBORING PROVINCE TO INQUIRE ABOUT HER PRESENT WHEREABOUTS.

WE ARE ALSO SEARCHING FOR A SAMURAI NAMED NATTO WHO MAY BE THE NEXT VICTIM.
WHAT MAKES YOU THINK THAT?

HE MAY HAVE BEEN THE ONE WHO ACTUALLY KILLED MERCHANT HAYATE.
HMM...DO YOU HAVE ANY LEADS AS TO HIS PRESENT LOCATION?
NONE.
AND THERE NEVER WILL BE WITHOUT THE CHAMBERLAIN'S COOPERATION.

HMM...VERY WELL. KEEP ME INFORMED OF YOUR PROGRESS.
IF YOU WISH.
22.

IS INSPECTOR OGAWA USUALLY INTERESTED IN YOUR CASES, IKEDA-SAN?
ON THE CONTRARY! NO DOUBT HE STILL HOPES TO GET THIS CASE REASSIGNED TO HIM.
THAT'S ENOUGH BUSINESS TALK! NOW ENJOY YOUR MEAL!
IT SMELLS DELICIOUS!
HA HA! AS YOU SAY, HARUKO!
I NOTICED SOME TOYS IN THE OTHER ROOM.
DO YOU HAVE A CHILD?
GASP!
.....
CRASH!
!
EX-EXCUSE ME, USAGI-SAN!
ER...OUR SON DIED OF AN ILLNESS LAST YEAR.
I-I'M SORRY. I DID NOT INTEND TO UPSET HER.
YOU COULD NOT HAVE KNOWN, MY FRIEND.
PARDON ME. I WILL LOOK IN ON MY WIFE.
23

USAGI! USAGI!

EH--?
USAGI, WAKE UP!
I'VE JUST BEEN INFORMED THAT ANOTHER BODY HAS BEEN DISCOVERED!

A FARMER CARTING HIS PRODUCE TO TOWN DISCOVERED AND REPORTED THE BODY EARLY THIS MORNING!
IS IT NATTO?

I DON'T KNOW... BUT WE'LL FIND OUT IN A MINUTE!

IT'S A **WOMAN**!
THIS IS MOST UNEXPECTED!
24.

HOW WAS SHE KILLED?
IT APPEARS IT WAS DONE WITH A BLADE.
THEN THIS HAS NO CONNECTION TO THE MURDERS OF THE THREE MERCHANTS.

SHE'S WEARING SOME RICE POWDER.
IT DOESN'T MEAN MUCH. MANY WOMEN WEAR IT AS MAKE-UP.

HAVE YOU FOUND OUT WHO SHE IS?
NO ONE AROUND HERE CAN IDENTIFY HER, INSPECTOR ISHIDA.
AKIMÉ!
25

AKIMÉ!
STOP!
LET THEM THROUGH!
DO YOU KNOW THIS WOMAN?

AKIMÉ!
WHO ARE YOU?

WE ARE FROM THE UNAGIYAMA ENTERTAINMENT TROUPE. THIS WOMAN IS--ER, WAS--A MEMBER OF OUR GROUP.

SHE'S DEAD! ARE YOU GOING TO FIND THE ONE RESPONSIBLE OR WILL YOU IGNORE HER MURDER BECAUSE WE'RE JUST ITINERANT ACTORS?!

WATCH WHAT YOU SAY, GOKU!
BAH! I KNOW HOW THEY OPERATE! MURDERERS WILL GO UNPUNISHED AROUND HERE!
WE WILL DO WHAT WE CAN, ACTOR!
26

IF YOU WON'T FIND AKIME'S KILLER, I'LL DO IT MYSELF!
IF YOU BREAK THE LAW, I'LL ARREST YOU!

WHAT'S GOING ON?!

CHIEF INSPECTOR OGAWA!
FOUR KILLINGS IN TWO DAYS?!
WHAT IS THIS TOWN COMING TO?
ANY MORE PAPERWORK AND I'LL BE TOO BUSY TO ENTERTAIN MY GUEST TONIGHT! HA HA!

WELL, AT LEAST THIS ONE DOESN'T LOOK LIKE SOMEBODY IMPORTANT!

WHAT?! WHY YOU--!
NO, GOKU! HE'S A COP!
TSK!
27.

YES, GOKU, ASSAULT ME AND ***YOU'LL*** BE THE ONE WHO IS ARRESTED! FOOL--I AM YOUR BETTER! UNDERSTAND?!
WELL, DO YOU?!

Y-YES... I UNDERSTAND.
GOOD. NOW GET OUT OF HERE! THIS IS A POLICE INVESTIGATION!

WE'LL CANCEL TONIGHT'S PERFORMANCE IN AKIME'S MEMORY, GOKU.
SNICKER!
WHAT A WORTHLESS FOOL!
YOU WERE TOO HARSH WITH HIM!

THAT'S HOW YOU TREAT RIFFRAFF! THEY HAVE TO BE MADE TO RESPECT AUTHORITY!
I SEE THE SAME FAILING IN YOU SOMETIMES, ISHIDA!
THANK YOU FOR THE CRITICISM, OGAWA-SAN.

I JUST BELIEVE THAT NO MATTER HOW LOW THEIR POSITION, EVERYONE IS ENTITLED TO JUSTICE.
HA HA! AN IDEALIST! YOU HAVE GOT TO LEARN HOW TO WORK IN THE REAL WORLD, ISHIDA!
28

YOU ALREADY HAVE YOUR HANDS FULL WITH INVESTIGATING THREE HOMICIDES. I WILL HANDLE THIS ONE MYSELF.
OF COURSE, INSPECTOR OGAWA. I CANNOT ARGUE WITH YOUR LOGIC.

I DON'T WANT TO KEEP YOU FROM YOUR OTHER DUTIES, ISHIDA.
YOU ARE TOO KIND, CHIEF INSPECTOR.
COME, USAGI-SAN.

I FEAR THE INVESTIGATION INTO HER DEATH ENDS HERE.
YOU'RE RIGHT. OGAWA KNEW I COULDN'T TAKE ON ANOTHER CASE. TO CHALLENGE HIM WOULD HAVE BEEN FUTILE.

THAT'S NOT WHAT OGAWA THINKS. IT SEEMS LIKE HE WANTED YOU TO DEFY HIM.
I DO HAVE A HISTORY OF BEING A BIT OF A REBEL, USAGI, BUT I CHOOSE MY BATTLES CAREFULLY.

HE IS AN INTOLERABLE PERSON.
YES. HE MAY BE CORRUPT, BUT HE IS STILL MY SUPERIOR AND I WILL NEVER GO AGAINST A SUPERIOR...

...UNLESS IT SERVES A GOOD PURPOSE.
HER MURDERER WILL BE FOUND, USAGI-SAN. THIS I SWEAR TO YOU.
29.

WHAT NOW? DO WE SEARCH FOR THAT *SAMURAI*-- NATTO?
CHAMBERLAIN TOYOFUKU WAS EVASIVE BUT ASSURED ME NATTO IS NO LONGER IN THIS AREA!

YOU SOUND AS IF YOU DOUBT THE CHAMBERLAIN'S HONESTY.
YOU KNOW HE WAS UNCOOPERATIVE AND WOULD NOT ALLOW US TO SEARCH THROUGH THE OFFICIAL RECORDS.

HOWEVER, I DID SEND OUT INQUIRIES LAST NIGHT AND THERE IS NO ONE BY THAT NAME IN TOWN.
SO THE CHAMBERLAIN WAS BEING TRUTHFUL?
THERE IS TRUTH AND THERE IS THE ***TRUTH,*** USAGI-SAN.

WELL, MAYBE HE JUST CHANGED HIS NAME.
IT IS NOT UNCOMMON FOR A *SAMURAI* TO DO SO IF THERE IS A CHANGE IN STATUS.
HMM...

YOU COULD BE RIGHT! THE THREE APPRENTICES BENEFITED BY MERCHANT HAYATE'S DEATH, WHY NOT THE *SAMURAI*?
30.

IN OUR CULTURE A FAMILY'S LINEAGE IS OF THE UTMOST IMPORTANCE. A CHANGE OF NAME WILL BE RECORDED.

WHERE WOULD THE RECORDS BE KEPT?

THERE...

...IN LORD YAMAHASHI'S ARCHIVES--THE VERY PLACE TO WHICH I WAS FORBIDDEN ACCESS!

BUT I AM DETERMINED TO SEE JUSTICE DONE.
COME ON!

IF LUCK IS ON OUR SIDE, WE'LL BE ABLE TO BLUFF OUR WAY.
31.

IN THE ARCHIVES...
YES? YES?! WHAT DO YOU WANT HERE?!
I AM INSPECTOR ISHIDA. I HAVE COME TO EXAMINE CERTAIN RECORDS--THOSE FIFTEEN YEARS PAST.
YOU CAN'T JUST COME IN HERE! YOU NEED AUTHORIZATION!
THIS *JITTÉ*, THE SYMBOL OF JUSTICE, GIVES ME THE AUTHORIZATION!
NOW, WHERE ARE THE RECORDS?!
ER...UH... OF COURSE. THE YEAR YOU WANT IS RIGHT HERE!
HE'S GOING TO REPORT US. WE HAD BETTER HURRY!
THE RECORDS ARE EVEN MORE COMPREHENSIVE THAN I EXPECTED! THIS MAY TAKE A WHILE!
32

AFTER A WHILE...
THIS MIGHT BE IT!
IT'S A LEDGER OF BIRTHS AND DEATHS...
...AND, PERHAPS, NAME CHANGES!

ISHIDA!

CH-CHAMBERLAIN TOYOFUKU--!
WHAT IS THE MEANING OF THIS UNAUTHORIZED SEARCH?!
I'VE ALREADY SENT A LETTER OF OBJECTION TO YOUR SUPERIOR! NOW I WILL SEE TO YOUR DEMOTION!
WELL, DID YOU FIND WHAT YOU WERE LOOKING FOR?
NO.
MY BOOKS!

BAH! I SHOULD HAVE YOU ARRESTED AND THROWN INTO YOUR OWN PRISON, BUT I WOULD RATHER AVOID A SCANDAL. NOW GET OUT OR I WILL DEMAND YOU EVEN PERFORM SEPPUKU* TO PAY FOR YOUR DISOBEDIENCE!
*RITUAL SUICIDE

ESCORT THEM TO THE CASTLE GATES! IF THEY SHOW UP AGAIN, KILL THEM!
33

WE WERE SO CLOSE! WE HAD THE DOCUMENT IN OUR HANDS! THERE IS NO HOPE OF FINDING THE TRUTH NOW!
I DON'T KNOW ABOUT THAT.

WHAT DO YOU MEAN?
SHH...

THE DOCUMENT?!

YOU DARED TO STEAL AN OFFICIAL DOCUMENT FROM LORD YAMAHASHI'S ARCHIVES?! DO YOU KNOW WHAT THE PENALTY FOR THAT IS?!

WELL, COME ON--WE'D BETTER GET IT OFF THE STREETS!
HURRY--WE DO NOT HAVE MUCH DAYLIGHT LEFT!
34

LATER...
HERE IT IS-- NATTO HIROSHI!
HE DID CHANGE HIS NAME--

--TO OGAWA!

CHIEF INSPECTOR OGAWA-- MY SUPERIOR!
CHAMBERLAIN TOYOFUKU SPONSORED HIM FOR HIS POSITION IN THE POLICE DEPARTMENT!

FOR HIM TO AWARD SUCH A KEY POST TO AN UNKNOWN IS SUSPICIOUS!
HE MUST HAVE BEEN ONE OF THOSE OGAWA BRIBED!

THAT'S WHY THE CHAMBERLAIN WAS SO UNCOOPERATIVE-- HE DID NOT WANT HIS CORRUPTION TO BE EXPOSED!
OGAWA COULD BE THE NEXT VICTIM!
AT THE LEAST, WE KNOW HIM TO BE A MURDERER!

HURRY-- WE'VE GOT TO GET TO THE POLICE STATION!
35

WHERE IS CHIEF INSPECTOR OGAWA?!
THE CHIEF INSPECTOR?
HE'S CHECKED OUT, SIR!
HE SAID HE WILL BE ENTERTAINING A GUEST TONIGHT!

GATHER ALL OUR AVAILABLE OFFICERS IN THE COURTYARD!
YES, SIR!
WHAT'S GOING ON?

INSPECTOR NII?! WHAT ARE YOU DOING HERE? I SENT YOU TO THE NEXT PROVINCE TO FIND OUT THE WHEREABOUTS OF MERCHANT HAYATE'S DAUGHTER AND SON!
YES, INSPECTOR ISHIDA! I DID GO!
ALL OFFICERS-- INTO THE COURTYARD IMMEDIATELY!

I RETURNED LATE LAST NIGHT, AND INSPECTOR OGAWA HAD ME REPORT TO HIM. HE SAID HE WOULD RELAY MY INFORMATION TO YOU HIMSELF. DIDN'T HE SEE YOU?!
36

WE SAW INSPECTOR OGAWA THIS MORNING, BUT HE SAID NOTHING.
WHAT DID YOU LEARN, NII?

MERCHANT HAYATE'S KIDS WERE **NOT** GIVEN TO RELATIVES. THEY WERE **SOLD** TO AN INNKEEPER IN THE NEXT PROVINCE.

FIVE YEARS AGO THEY WERE RESOLD TO A TRAVELING ENTERTAINMENT TROUPE.
THERE'S ONE IN TOWN NOW!
IT HAS TO BE MORE THAN MERE COINCIDENCE!

THE DEAD WOMAN THIS MORNING--SHE WAS HAYATE'S DAUGHTER!
SHE'S ABOUT THE RIGHT AGE.

OGAWA MUST HAVE KILLED HER AFTER NII REPORTED TO HIM! THAT'S THE REAL REASON HE TOOK OVER THE INVESTIGATION!
I SUSPECT IT HAS ALREADY BEEN CLOSED.
37.

THE OFFICERS ARE ASSEMBLED IN THE COURTYARD, SIR!
WHO ARE WE GOING TO ARREST?!

INSPECTOR OGAWA.
B-BUT, SIR--! IS IT POSSIBLE?! HE IS THE *SENIOR OFFICER!*

HARUMPH! DO I NEED TO REMIND YOU, NII, THAT WE ARE DEFENDERS OF JUSTICE? NO ONE IS BEYOND THE LAW. IT IS OUR DUTY TO METE OUT JUSTICE IMPARTIALLY!
UNDERSTAND?!
Y-YES, SIR!

GOOD. NOW FOLLOW ME. WE GO TO ARREST A MURDERER!
GULP! YES, INSPECTOR ISHIDA!

38

COME, MY DEAR, POUR ME MORE SAKE!

CERTAINLY, SIR!
AHH... IT ALWAYS TASTES SWEETER WHEN POURED BY A BEAUTIFUL WOMAN.

OH, YOU'RE SUCH A FLATTERER!
SLURP! AHH...
HERE, LET ME POUR YOU ANOTHER.
SURE. AFTER ALL, THIS IS A CELEBRATION OF SORTS, YOU KNOW.

REALLY? WHAT ARE YOU CELEBRATING, MY LORD?
"MY LORD"? HA! I LIKE THAT!
IT FITS ME!

I'VE OUTLIVED ALL MY FOES-- THREE MERCHANTS WHO, SOMEDAY, COULD HAVE PROVEN TO BE A THREAT...

...EVEN AN UNEXPECTED ENEMY WAS TAKEN CARE OF LAST NIGHT!
HA!
SLURP!

AND THERE'S JUST ONE MORE-- A COLLEAGUE, YOU KNOW. HE'S TOO HEADSTRONG, POKING HIS NOSE INTO MY BUSINESS. ONCE I HAVE HIM THROWN OFF THE FORCE, MY SECRETS WILL BE SAFE!
AHH...
37

HERE. DRINK MORE. A VIRILE MAN LIKE YOURSELF CAN HANDLE IT!
HA HA! NOW WHO IS THE FLATTERER?!

YOU REALLY ARE A PRETTY THING! I'M GLAD THE LOTUS HOUSE SENT YOU. YOUR BEAUTY MUST EVEN RIVAL LADY MAPLE HERSELF!

"THE LOTUS HOUSE"? OH, NO, MY LORD, I AM NOT FROM THAT ESTABLISHMENT. I INTERCEPTED THEIR COURTESAN AND SENT HER BACK...

...AND I CAME HERE IN HER PLACE.
WH-WHAT--?! BUT I DON'T UNDERSTAND...

THEN UNDERSTAND THIS, MURDERER!
EYAHH!
40

YAHH! NO--I KILLED YOU!
ULP!
THUNK!

KILLED ME?! NO...BUT YOU SLEW MY FATHER AND MY MOTHER...

...AND MY SISTER!
A MAN?!

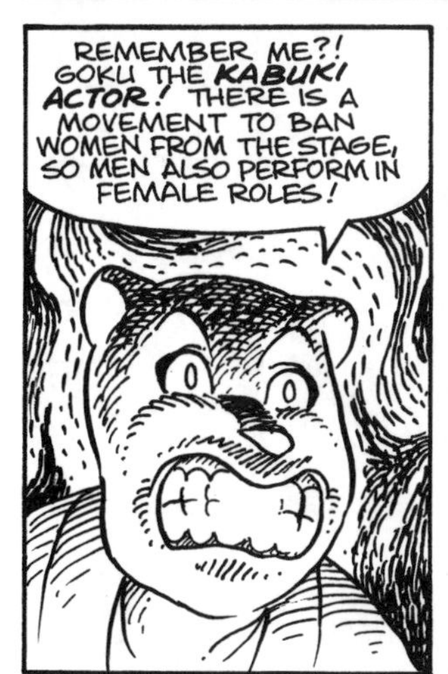
REMEMBER ME?! GOKU THE KABUKI ACTOR! THERE IS A MOVEMENT TO BAN WOMEN FROM THE STAGE, SO MEN ALSO PERFORM IN FEMALE ROLES!

Y-YOU'RE HAYATE'S SON!

YOU GAINED YOUR POSITION FROM THE DEATHS OF MY PARENTS AND KEPT IT WITH THE MURDER OF MY SISTER!

41

YOU SHOULD HAVE KILLED MY SISTER AND ME WITH OUR PARENTS, BUT YOUR GREED WAS GREAT! YOU WERE NOT CONTENT WITH STEALING MY FATHER'S GOLD. YOU SOLD US, THINKING WE WOULD NEVER BE A THREAT TO YOU!
I SAW YOU KILL MY PARENTS. I WAS YOUNG, BUT YOUR IMAGE WAS BURNED IN MY MEMORY!
YOUR ACCOMPLICES WERE SIMPLE TO FIND! AFTER ALL, THEY WERE PROMINENT BUSINESSMEN.
DRESSED IN MY COSTUME, IT WAS SO EASY TO GET CLOSE TO THEM! THEY WERE SO UNSUSPECTING!
BUT YOU -- HAVING CHANGED YOUR IDENTITY -- I COULD NOT LOCATE! I RECOGNIZED YOU THIS MORNING AND WAS DUMBFOUNDED BY MY LUCK!
YOU WERE INVISIBLE TO ME UNTIL YOU KILLED AKIME! YOUR OWN ACTIONS BROUGHT YOU TO ME! IT IS KARMA, NEH?
NOW I'LL KILL YOU!
92

I SHOULD HAVE KILLED YOU WITH YOUR PARENTS!

EYAHH!
SHUK!

DIE!

NO! NO! YAHHH!!
INSPECTOR OGAWA!
STOP HIM!
DIE, MONSTER!

NOOo--!
GYAHH!
KIYAHH!
43.

ISHIDA--! Y-YOU GOT HERE JUST IN TIME! YOU SAVED MY LIFE! I-I--
UNHAND ME!
WHA--?!

I'VE COME TO ARREST YOU, NOT RESCUE YOU--THE MURDERS OF MERCHANT HAYATE...HIS WIFE...HIS DAUGHTER! I'LL SEE YOU PUNISHED FOR YOUR CRIMES!
WH-WHAT?!
WHY YOU--!

HOW DARE YOU SPEAK TO YOUR SUPERIOR THAT WAY--YOU WITH YOUR IDEALIZED NOTION OF JUSTICE!

ALL OF YOU--*OUT!* I WANT TO TALK TO THIS UPSTART IN PRIVATE! OUT!
YOU TOO, YOU LONG-EARED MEDDLER!

I DON'T KNOW WHAT YOU *THINK* YOU'VE UNCOVERED ABOUT ME, ISHIDA, BUT I WON'T BE FOUND GUILTY OF ANY CRIME, NO MATTER HOW MUCH EVIDENCE YOU HAVE!

YOU, ON THE OTHER HAND, ARE A DIFFERENT MATTER! I KNOW YOU'VE BROUGHT THAT LONG-EARED *RONIN* ON THIS CASE WITHOUT AUTHORIZATION! I'LL HAVE YOU DISMISSED FROM THE FORCE FOR THAT!
44

YES, I ADMIT IT--I'M RESPONSIBLE FOR THOSE CRIMES. BUT THEY WERE INSIGNIFICANT LIVES. DO YOU REALLY BELIEVE I WILL BE PUNISHED?!
I HAVE TOO MANY INFLUENTIAL FRIENDS--CHAMBELAIN TOYOFUKU, HIMSELF, WILL SPEAK ON MY BEHALF!
YOU REALLY ARE NAIVE IF YOU THINK THE LAW APPLIES TO EVERYONE! IN THIS CASE THE GUILTY WILL GO FREE AND THE VICTIMS WILL LIE UNMOURNED AND UNAVENGED!
WHERE IS YOUR JUSTICE NOW, ISHIDA?!

EEEEYAHHHHH---!

INSPECTOR!
FOOLS! GOKU WAS NOT YET DEAD!
HE PICKED UP A SWORD AND KILLED INSPECTOR OGAWA WITH HIS LAST BREATH!
45

LATER...
A TRAGEDY.
BUT ONE THING PUZZLES ME.
WHAT'S THAT, USAGI?

I EXAMINED GOKU MYSELF. I HAVE SEEN DEATH ENOUGH TIMES TO KNOW THAT HE WAS NOT ALIVE.
REALLY? YOU COULD HAVE BEEN MISTAKEN.

ER...YES. PERHAPS SO.
WELL, THE RECORDS WILL SHOW THAT GOKU EXACTED REVENGE FOR THE MURDER OF HIS FAMILY WITH HIS DYING BREATH.
JUSTICE HAS BEEN SERVED.

EVEN IF IT WAS *HELPED* A LITTLE?

I DON'T KNOW WHAT YOU'RE INSINUATING, USAGI-SAN.

EARLY THE NEXT MORNING...

AH, GOOD MORNING, INSPECTOR ISHIDA! YOU LOOK TIRED.
THERE ARE MANY LOOSE ENDS TO TIE UP WITH THE CLOSING OF THIS CASE.
I CAN IMAGINE!

UNFORTUNATELY, OGAWA'S CRIMES WILL BE COVERED UP BECAUSE OF HIS CONNECTION TO CHAMBERLAIN TOYOFUKU AND OTHERS.

HOWEVER, IN RETURN FOR MY SILENCE, THE CHAMBERLAIN HAS ACCEPTED THE RETURN OF THE STOLEN RECORDS WITH NO QUESTIONS ASKED.
THAT IS A RELIEF!
WELL, AT LEAST JUSTICE WAS SERVED.

HERE IS THE REWARD FOR BANDIT HOSOKU THAT YOU FIRST CAME TO SEE ME ABOUT. IT WAS APPROVED THIS MORNING.
THANK YOU.

WELL, WITH THE HAIRPIN MURDERS SOLVED, I'M FREE THIS AFTERNOON. WOULD YOU LIKE TO BE MY GUEST TO SEE THE KABUKI?
WHERE MEN PLAY FEMALE ROLES? SURE. I'D BETTER SEE IT NOW. AFTER ALL, IT'S PROBABLY JUST A FAD THAT WILL DIE OUT IN A FEW YEARS!
HA! HA! HA! HA! HA!
47

HEY--! WATCH OUT, GIRL!

OH--!

WHERE IS SHE?! DON'T TELL ME WE LOST HER!
FIND HER OR OUR HEADS WILL BE FORFEIT!
I THINK I SEE HER IN THAT CROWD!

THAT'S NOT HER!
QUICK-- BACK TO WHERE WE LAST SAW HER!

SEARCH THE CROWDS!

WE'VE LOST HER!
WE'LL FIND HER AGAIN!

THE END.

the Courtesan
1.

IT'S HER AGAIN--SHE LOOKS LIKE SHE'S IN A HURRY.
I HOPE SHE'S NOT IN ANY TROUBLE.

SO--WE'VE CAUGHT YOU AT LAST! NOW YOU'LL TELL US WHERE HE IS!
LET ME GO!
UH-OH--WE'VE BEEN SEEN!
WHAT'S GOING ON?
RELEASE HER!
WHO ARE YOU?!
2.

KILL THE MEDDLER!
KIYAHH!

URK!

GYAK!

THOSE INCOMPETENTS--! I'LL HAVE TO HANDLE HIM MYSELF!
URK!
OOF!

EYARK!

I AM MIYAMOTO USAGI. ARE YOU ALL RIGHT?
Y-YES. THANK YOU, USAGI-SAN.

I BUMPED INTO YOU THE OTHER NIGHT. YOU SEEMED AFRAID. WAS IT THESE MEN YOU WERE IN FEAR OF? IS THERE ANYTHING I CAN DO?

I HAVE ALREADY BEEN A GREAT IMPOSITION TO YOU. I MUST BE GOING. FORGIVE ME THAT I CANNOT THANK YOU PROPERLY.
AT LEAST LET ME SEE YOU TO YOUR DESTINATION SAFELY.

NO! AND YOU MUST GIVE ME YOUR WORD OF HONOR THAT YOU WILL NOT FOLLOW ME!
VERY WELL. I SHOULD REPORT THESE DEATHS, ANYWAY!

NO. LEAVE THEM. THERE ARE TOO MANY QUESTIONS TO WHICH YOU DO NOT KNOW THE ANSWERS...
...AND I AM UNABLE TO SUPPLY THEM.

SHE MAY BE RIGHT. THESE ARE NOT ORDINARY THIEVES.
4.

ARE YOU ENJOYING YOUR BREAKFAST, SAMURAI?

UH... YES, IT'S... DELICIOUS.

HEY, EVERYBODY--! YOU'VE GOT TO SEE THIS!
WHAT IS IT?

LADY MAPLE, THE BEAUTIFUL COURTESAN, IS LEADING HER PROCESSION THROUGH TOWN!
WOW! I'VE GOT TO SEE THAT!
ME, TOO!
WAIT FOR ME!

SHE'S ALMOST HERE!
WHAT'S THE BIG COMMOTION ALL ABOUT?
LOOK! LOOK! THERE SHE IS!
HOW BEAUTIFUL SHE IS!

AH--!
5

THEY SAY EVEN LORD YAMAHASHI GOES TO SEE HER.
YEAH, BUT THAT WAS BEFORE HIS HEALTH STARTED FAILING.
OF COURSE!
STEP ASIDE FOR THE PROCESSION OF LADY MAPLE!
PLEASE PATRONIZE THE LOTUS HOUSE!

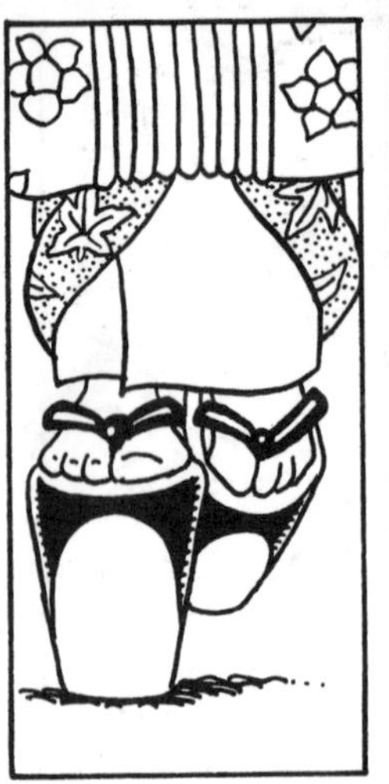

SH-SHE'S BEAUTIFUL!
6.

SHE REALLY IS SOMETHING, ISN'T SHE?

GULP!

AH--!
7.

SIGH...
D-DID YOU SEE THAT?! SHE SMILED AT ME!
NO SHE DIDN'T! SHE SMILED AT ME!
WHY WOULD SHE SMILE AT YOUR UGLY FACE?!
IT WAS ME SHE SMILED AT! ME! ME!
8.

THAT EVENING...

I HOPE DINNER TASTES BETTER THAN BREAKFAST DID.

ULP! NOT MUCH BETTER!
AT LEAST IT'S CHEAP!

USAGI-SAN--! A MESSENGER HAS JUST DELIVERED A LETTER FOR YOU!
IT'S A TENBENI!
A WHAT?
YOU REALLY ARE NAIVE, AREN'T YOU?!

IT'S A LETTER FROM A COURTESAN! SEE-- THE PAPER'S EDGE IS RED.
WHERE? LET ME SEE THAT!
WHY WOULD I RECEIVE SUCH A LETTER?

HEY!
WOW! IT'S FROM LADY MAPLE HERSELF!
GIVE ME THAT!
9.

SHE WANTS TO SEE ME!
IT'S SUCH AN HONOR!
WHY WOULD SHE WANT TO SEE *YOU?*
I'M HANDSOMER!
HOMELIER, YOU MEAN!
HAHAHAHAHAHAHA

WHERE CAN I FIND THE LOTUS HOUSE?
GO DOWN THIS STREET, THEN ASK DIRECTIONS. ANYONE CAN TELL YOU THE WAY!
HEY, SAMURAI!

TAKE ME ALONG, HUH?
YEAH, ME, TOO!
SORRY. THE INVITATION'S FOR ME ONLY.

WHY DID LADY MAPLE INVITE *HIM?*
WHY NOT ONE OF US?
I GUESS THERE'S NO ACCOUNTING FOR TASTE.
EVEN WITH A BEAUTIFUL WOMAN!
10

THIS MUST BE IT! IT TRULY IS AN IMPRESSIVE PLACE.

EXCUSE ME. I AM MIYAMOTO USAGI. I RECEIVED THIS LETTER...
AH, OF COURSE, USAGI-SAN! LADY MAPLE HAS BEEN ANXIOUSLY AWAITING YOU.

BUT I REALLY DON'T KNOW WHY SHE--
I'M SURE SHE WILL EXPLAIN EVERYTHING TO YOU, USAGI-SAN.

THIS IS HER PRIVATE COMPOUND...PLEASE WATCH YOUR HEAD.
HER "PRIVATE COMPOUND"--?

LADY MAPLE, USAGI-SAN IS HERE.
PLEASE GO RIGHT IN, SIR.
UH... THANK YOU.
11.

IT PLEASES ME THAT YOU CHOSE TO ACCEPT MY MODEST INVITATION, USAGI-SAN. WELCOME.
SHE'S SO BEAUTIFUL!
PLEASE BE SEATED.

YOU SEEM A LITTLE DISTRAUGHT, USAGI-SAN. IS THERE SOMETHING THE MATTER?

HUH? UH--NO, NO, LADY MAPLE... ER... YOUR LADYSHIP... UH... IT'S JUST THAT THERE MUST BE SOME MISTAKE... YOU SEE, I...

NO, I AM SURE THERE IS NO MISTAKE. AND, PLEASE, I WOULD LIKE IT IF YOU SIMPLY CALLED ME "MAPLE."
YOSHINO, WOULD YOU SERVE US SOME TEA?
YES, LADY MAPLE.

YOU!
YES. I SERVE LADY MAPLE.
WELL, I'M GLAD TO SEE THAT YOU'RE ALL RIGHT!
12.

I ASKED YOU HERE TO THANK YOU, USAGI-SAN, FOR A SERVICE YOU HAVE RENDERED ME.
THANK YOU, YOSHINO.
YOU'RE WELCOME, LADY MAPLE.

YOSHINO SAYS YOU SAVED HER FROM SOME THIEVES WHILE SHE WAS OUT ON AN ERRAND FOR ME LAST NIGHT.
IT WOULD BE IMPOLITE NOT TO COMPENSATE YOU IN SOME WAY.

PLEASE... STAY AT THE LOTUS HOUSE AS MY GUEST, USAGI-SAN. YOU'LL FIND IT MUCH MORE COMFORTABLE THAN THE INN YOU ARE PRESENTLY STAYING AT.
PLEASE STAY, USAGI-SAN.
ME? HERE--? UH... UH...

THAT IS A MOST GENEROUS OFFER, LADY... ER... MAPLE... BUT I... JUST COULDN'T IMPOSE. THAT IS, I...

IT IS NO IMPOSITION, I ASSURE YOU. WE HAVE THE MOST COMFORTABLE ROOMS, THE FINEST COOKS--

OKAY.
13

I WILL SHOW YOU TO YOUR ROOM, USAGI-SAN.
THANK YOU, YOSHINO-SAN.

LADY MAPLE IS VERY GRACIOUS.
WELL, UH...
YOU MEAN **BEAUTIFUL,** DON'T YOU? THAT IS WHAT MEN NOTICE FIRST.
HA HA! NO NEED TO BE EMBARRASSED, USAGI-SAN. IT'S TRUE!

BUT YOU'RE RIGHT.
SHE IS GOOD-HEARTED. THAT IS HER NATURE.
HER "*NATURE*"?

YES. BY RESCUING ME, YOU RENDERED HER A SERVICE, HOWEVER UNKNOWINGLY. SHE FEELS IT IS HER OBLIGATION TO REPAY YOU.

THAT IS UNNECESSARY.
PERHAPS. BUT SHE BELIEVES OTHERWISE.
A REMARKABLE PERSON!

YES. I WOULD WILLINGLY EVEN GIVE MY LIFE FOR HER.
HERE IS YOUR ROOM. A MAID WILL BE ASSIGNED TO SEE TO YOUR NEEDS.
THANK YOU. IT LOOKS VERY COMFORTABLE.
14.

LATER THAT NIGHT...
:SIGH!: SUCH A DELICIOUS MEAL...

I HAVE TO ADMIT, THIS IS SO MUCH BETTER THAN THE INN I WAS STAYING AT.

IT'S A BEAUTIFUL NIGHT.
I THINK I'LL TAKE A WALK AROUND THE GROUNDS BEFORE TURNING IN.

:KEEEK!:
EH--?
IT APPEARS SOMEONE ELSE IS ENJOYING THE NIGHT AIR.

KEEEK!
IT'S YOSHINO! SHE MUST BE GOING OUT ON ANOTHER ERRAND FOR LADY MAPLE!

SHE COULD BE IN DANGER AGAIN.
BUT IT IS NONE OF MY BUSINESS.
BESIDES, I GAVE HER MY WORD THAT I WOULD NOT FOLLOW HER.

WELL, I'LL KEEP OUT OF HER SIGHT.
THERE'LL BE NO HARM DONE IF NOTHING HAPPENS.
15

THERE SHE GOES--INTO THAT SHOP.

THAT DIDN'T TAKE LONG.

SHE IS BEING FOLLOWED! I'D BETTER--! WAIT A MINUTE!

HER WALK IS SLIGHTLY DIFFERENT! IT'S NOT HER! CLEVER GIRL HIRED A STAND-IN! SHE SEEMS TO HAVE HIM FOOLED! HE'S FOLLOWING HER!

A SHORT WHILE LATER...
THERE'S THE REAL YOSHINO!

SHAY, LADY--Y'WANNA DRINK, HUH? HUH? :HIC!:
C'MON! DRINK WI' ME! :HICCUP!:
16.

SHE KEEPS LOOKING BEHIND HER...STOPPING AND LISTENING...DOUBLING BACK... SHE'S TAKING PAINS NOT TO BE FOLLOWED.
AT LEAST THAT DRUNK FINALLY LEFT HER ALONE!
THIS IS A WAREHOUSE AREA--NOT MANY PEOPLE AROUND HERE AT THIS TIME OF NIGHT.
WHAT COULD SHE BE DOING HERE?

IT LOOKS LIKE SHE'S REACHED HER DESTINATION.

IT SEEMS QUIET ENOUGH, BUT I'D BETTER WAIT OUT HERE FOR A WHILE IN CASE SHE NEEDS ME.

!

17.

THERE--! I'M SURE SHE WENT THIS WAY!
THEY'RE COMING!
THAT DRUNK WAS ONE OF THEM! I SHOULD HAVE SUSPECTED IT!
THEY'RE SMARTER THAN I THOUGHT...
...OR MAYBE I'M DUMBER THAN I THINK!

YOSHINO--YOU'VE GOT TO GET OUT OF HERE!

USAGI--?!
WHAT?!
18.

WHAT IS THE MEANING OF THIS?

SAMURAI, DRESSED LIKE THOSE WHO ATTACKED YOU, ARE COMING UP THE ROAD!
WHAT?!

YES. I SEE THEM.
WE'VE BEEN DISCOVERED!

USAGI-- TAKE KOTARO AND GO!
BUT... WHAT IS THIS ALL ABOUT?!

I CAN'T EXPLAIN, BUT THIS CHILD'S LIFE IS AT STAKE!
WHAT ABOUT YOU?
BLXT?

DON'T WORRY ABOUT CHIYO AND ME! DO AS I SAY--TAKE HIM SOMEWHERE SAFE, THEN GO TO LADY MAPLE AND TELL HER WHAT HAS HAPPENED!
GLBX?
19.

I WON'T LEAVE WITHOUT YOU!
WE'LL BE FINE. IT IS KOTARO THEY WANT!

BUT...
PLEASE-- DO AS I ASK.

AND SO...

WE JUST MADE IT!
CIRCLE THE BUILDING! MAKE SURE NO ONE ESCAPES!
20.

WE MUST GIVE USAGI-SAN TIME TO GET AWAY!
YES, YOSHINO-SAN. I WILL NOT FAIL YOU.

BREAK DOWN THE DOOR!

LOOK! THERE THEY GO!
AFTER THEM!
THEY GOT OUT A BACK WAY--AND THEY'RE CARRYING THE CHILD!

THEY'VE SEEN US! RUN, YOSHINO-SAN, RUN!

GET THEM!
DON'T LET THEM ESCAPE!
21

CHIYO, HURRY!
KEEP GOING, YOSHINO-SAN! KEEP GOING!

RUN, YOSHINO-SAN, RUN!
WHA--?!

EYAH!
OLD FOOL!

CHIYO!

OH--!
GOT YOU!
22.

WHAT DO WE DO WITH THIS ONE?
WE'VE GOT THE BOY. WE DON'T NEED HER.
KILL HER!
HOLD IT!
THIS IS JUST A BUNDLE OF RAGS!
WHAT?

WE'VE SEARCHED THE HOUSE!
IT'S EMPTY!
BUT THERE ARE SIGNS THERE WAS A CHILD IN THERE!

WHERE IS HE?!
I DON'T KNOW WHAT YOU'RE TALKING ABOUT!
BAH! TAKE HER WITH US!
SHE'LL SOON TELL US EVERYTHING WE WANT TO KNOW!

THEY ACTED AS DECOYS SO WE COULD ESCAPE!
WHEE GLXP!
COME ON, YOU!
I CAN'T JUST STAND HERE AND LET THEM TAKE HER!
23

!
USAGI--!

CLIK!
YAWN!

NO, USAGI, NO!
COME ON!

YAWN!
SMAK SMAK
NNN ZZZZ...

SIGH... SHE'S RIGHT! THEY SACRIFICED THEMSELVES SO I COULD GET AWAY WITH THIS CHILD.
ZZZ...
CLIK!

WHO ARE YOU?
ZZZ...

ZZZ...

END OF PART 1

SNIFF!
SNIFF!

the Courtesan
Part 2
EEP?
YEEEK!
1.

I NEED TO SEE LADY MAPLE!
THAT IS NOT POSSIBLE, USAGI-SAN. SHE IS WITH MERCHANT ODO.

PLEASE-- IT IS A MATTER OF UTMOST IMPORTANCE!
WELL... YOU ARE HER GUEST...
VERY WELL.

PLEASE WAIT IN HERE, AND I WILL TELL LADY MAPLE YOU WISH TO SEE HER.
THANK YOU.
MEANWHILE, I WILL HAVE SOME TEA BROUGHT IN TO YOU.

2.

SOON...
DID HE GIVE ANY INDICATION AS TO WHAT THIS IS ABOUT, SEI-CHAN?
NO, LADY MAPLE, BUT HE SEEMED AWFULLY AGITATED.
HMM... THAT SEEMS VERY UNLIKE HIM.

USAGI-SAN?
I NEED TO SPEAK TO YOU PRIVATELY, LADY MAPLE!
LADY MAPLE...?

IT'S ALL RIGHT, SEI-CHAN. PLEASE MAKE MY APOLOGIES TO MERCHANT ODO, AND INFORM HIM THAT I WILL BE INDISPOSED FOR A FEW MINUTES.
YES, LADY MAPLE.

NOW, USAGI-SAN. WHAT IS THIS ALL ABOUT?
FORGIVE ME, BUT I THOUGHT THIS MATTER REQUIRED GREAT PRIVACY.
ALLOW ME TO POUR YOU SOME TEA AS WE TALK.
3

I SAW YOSHINO LEAVE TONIGHT. I FEARED FOR HER SAFETY SO I FOLLOWED HER.

I AM DISAPPOINTED, USAGI-SAN.
THAT GOES BEYOND THE BOUNDARIES OF A GOOD GUEST.
I-I KNOW, BUT...

THEY TOOK HER!
!

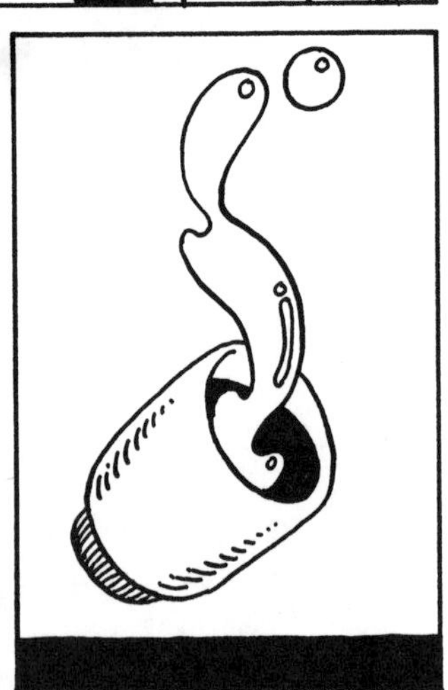

WHAT OF KOTARO?! DO THEY HAVE HIM AS WELL?
THE CHILD? NO. HE IS SAFE!
PRAISE THE GODS!
4.

WHERE IS HE?! YOU DIDN'T BRING HIM HERE--?
NO. HE IS SAFE AND WILL BE UNHARMED.
WE SHOULD BRING IN THE POLICE.
NO! WE CANNOT!

I WOULD LIKE TO HELP YOU, LADY MAPLE. TELL ME WHAT IS GOING ON. WHO ARE THOSE MASKED SAMURAI? WHO IS KOTARO?

THANK YOU, USAGI-SAN, BUT I AM RELUCTANT TO INVOLVE YOU IN MY PROBLEMS.

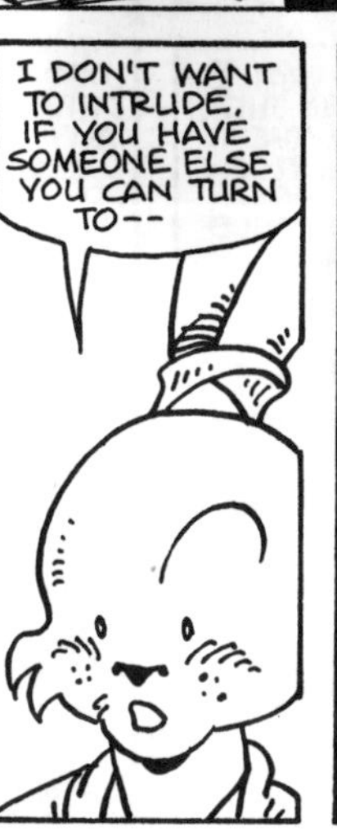
I DON'T WANT TO INTRUDE, IF YOU HAVE SOMEONE ELSE YOU CAN TURN TO--

SEI-CHAN, HAVE YOU RETURNED?
YES, LADY MAPLE.

GIVE MERCHANT ODO MY REGRETS. I WILL BE OCCUPIED FOR THE DURATION OF THE NIGHT...AND PLEASE SEE THAT WE ARE NOT DISTURBED.
YES, LADY MAPLE.

IT HAS BEEN SO LONG SINCE I TOLD SOMEONE THE STORY...LET ME START AT THE BEGINNING.
5

MY STORY BEGINS OH-SO-MANY YEARS AGO. I WAS THE YOUNGEST DAUGHTER TO A *SAMURAI* FAMILY.
OUR LORD HAD LOST THE WAR AND WE WERE DESTITUTE. FOR THE SURVIVAL OF THE FAMILY, MY PARENTS DID WHAT SO MANY OTHERS HAVE DONE IN SIMILAR CIRCUMSTANCES. I WAS SOLD TO ONE OF THE PLEASURE HOUSES OF THE CITY.

I WORKED AS KITCHEN HELP, THEN AS A MAID, WITHOUT COMPLAINT--AFTER ALL, I WAS THE DAUGHTER OF A *SAMURAI*.

THE MOST I COULD HOPE FOR IN ADULTHOOD WAS TO REMAIN A MAID OR BECOME A SECOND-CLASS PROSTITUTE... BUT I WAS ONE IN A THOUSAND. THE OWNERS OF THE HOUSE SAW SOME SPARK IN ME AND TRAINED ME AS AN *OIRAN*--A FIRST-CLASS COURTESAN.

I HAVE BEEN TOLD THAT I RIVAL EVEN THOSE IN THE FINEST HOUSES OF THE YOSHIWARA DISTRICT OF EDO. ONLY THE MOST PROMINENT OF MEN COULD AFFORD MY FAVORS.

LORD YAMAHASHI HIMSELF OFTEN CAME TO VISIT ME--ALWAYS IN DISGUISE, OF COURSE, AS IS ONLY PROPER FOR ONE OF HIS STATION. I BECAME HIS EXCLUSIVELY, AND, SOON, I WAS WITH CHILD... A LORD'S CHILD!

WE KEPT IT A SECRET FROM ALL BUT A TRUSTED FEW. I WENT INTO SECLUSION TO HAVE THE BABY, THOUGH PUBLICLY I WAS ON A TEMPLE PILGRIMAGE.

BUT THERE WERE RUMORS... AND THE LORD HAS MANY ENEMIES EVEN IN HIS OWN COUNCIL. SO, FOR SAFETY, I SENT MY CHILD, KOTARO, INTO HIDING WITH A NURSE. YOSHINO WAS MY ONLY CONTACT WITH MY SON.

6.

NOW LORD YAMAHASHI IS ILL--SOME SAY HE IS DYING. CHAMBERLAIN TOYOFUKU AND THE COUNCIL HAVE ASSUMED HIS DUTIES.

THE CHAMBERLAIN IS RELATED TO MY LORD, AND I FEAR HE IS BEHIND A CONSPIRACY TO MURDER MY CHILD.
BUT WHY?

HE FEARS KOTARO BECAUSE MY SON IS THE ONE, TRUE HEIR.

SEE THIS FAN? I CARRY IT WITH ME ALWAYS. THESE ARE KOTARO'S FOOTPRINTS, AND, WITH HIS OWN HANDS, LORD YAMAHASHI ACKNOWLEDGED KOTARO AS HIS SON!

KOTARO IS THE ONLY THING THAT STANDS BETWEEN CHAMBERLAIN TOYOFUKU AND THE THRONE.
IF KOTARO BECAME LORD, HE WOULD RULE BACKED BY A BOARD OF REGENTS.

BUT I DON'T WANT HIM TO BE A LORD. I AM MISSING KOTARO'S CHILDHOOD BECAUSE HE WAS BORN THE SON OF A LORD. I JUST WANT HIM TO BE A CHILD--MY CHILD--TO HOLD AND TO LOVE. IS THAT SO WRONG, USAGI-SAN?
NO.
7.

"DO YOU KNOW WHERE THE HOODED ONES HAVE TAKEN YOSHINO, LADY MAPLE?"
"NO... BUT I FEAR WHAT THEY MAY BE DOING TO HER!"
WHACK!
UH!

SWISHHH!

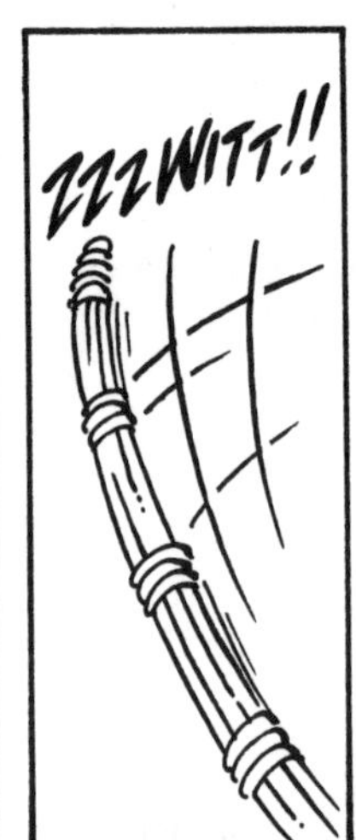
ZZZWITT!!

WHAK!
UH--!

WHERE IS HE?!
WHERE IS THE CHILD?!

I-I DON'T KNOW...

UH--!
WHACK!

SPEAK OR I'LL HAVE THE SKIN FLAYED OFF YOUR BODY!
I-I KNOW NOTHING...
LIAR!
ANSWER CHAMBERLAIN TOYOFUKU!
8.

WHERE IS HE?
BEAT HER AGAIN!

N-NO...PLEASE...I DON'T...KNOW WHERE HE IS...
I-I... GAVE HIM...TO A SAMURAI...TO TAKE TO... SAFETY...

BAH! SHE'S FAINTED.
SHE COULD BE TELLING THE TRUTH. OUR AGENTS REPORT A LONG-EARED SAMURAI STAYING AT THE LOTUS HOUSE--A GUEST OF LADY MAPLE, NO LESS.

A SAMURAI, EH? HE PROBABLY HAS THE KID IN HIDING. LORD YAMAHASHI'S HEALTH IS FADING RAPIDLY. WE HAVEN'T MUCH TIME, SO WE'RE FORCED TO TAKE DIRECT ACTION.

GATHER ALL OUR MEN.
WE MAY NEED HER LATER...
...CUT HER DOWN.
YES, SIR!
9.

I HAVE NO IDEA WHERE YOSHINO COULD BE. I CAN ONLY KEEP MY EYES OPEN FOR THOSE HOODED *SAMURAI*.
THAT'S THE HOME THAT SHE WAS TAKEN FROM. IT'S AS GOOD A PLACE AS ANY TO START.

WHAT A MESS. THEY WERE THOROUGH IN THEIR SEARCH.

THEY HAVE YOSHINO... BUT SHE CAN'T TELL THEM WHERE THE CHILD IS.
WHAT WOULD I DO IN THEIR PLACE?

THEY MUST KNOW I HAVE KOTARO.
BUT THEY DON'T KNOW WHO I AM... ONLY THAT I AM STAYING AT--

!

WHAT A FOOL I AM!
10

SOON...
SEI-CHAN... WHAT HAPPENED HERE?!
OH, USAGI-SAN! IT WAS TERRIBLE!
NOTHING LIKE THIS HAS EVER HAPPENED BEFORE!

A GANG OF HOODED BRIGANDS ATTACKED THE LOTUS HOUSE--THEY KIDNAPPED LADY MAPLE! SAVE HER, USAGI-SAN! SAVE HER!

THAT SETTLES IT...I'VE GOT TO TELL THE POLICE WHAT I KNOW.
SAMURAI!
WHO? ME?

I WAS PAID TWO ZENI TO DELIVER THIS TO THE LONG-EARED SAMURAI STAYING AT THE LOTUS HOUSE.
THAT WOULD BE ME.
WHAT DOES IT SAY, USAGI-SAN?

"BRING THE BOY TO THE TORII GATE SOUTH OF TOWN AT SUNRISE OR LADY MAPLE DIES! COME ALONE."
I CAN'T BRING IN THE POLICE NOW!
11.

YOU'RE A COWARD, CHAMBERLAIN TOYOFUKU, TO PLOT TO MURDER A CHILD!
HE IS NOT A CHILD, LADY MAPLE! HE IS AN OBSTACLE TO MY POWER!
THE SUN IS RISING. THE *SAMURAI* SHOULD BE HERE SOON.

DO YOU THINK USAGI-SAN WILL COME, LADY MAPLE?
I PRAY HE WILL NOT, YOSHINO.
QUIET, YOU TWO! IF HE ISN'T HERE SOON, WE'LL SEND YOUR HEADS TO THE LOTUS HOUSE!

LEAVE KOTARO ALONE, CHAMBERLAIN TOYOFUKU! I SWEAR WE WILL LEAVE THIS AREA AND NEVER RETURN!
DO YOU THINK I WILL TAKE YOUR WORD? YOUR SON IS A THREAT AS LONG AS HE LIVES!

BRR... I HOPE SOMETHING HAPPENS SOON... I'M FREEZING OUT HERE.
THAT *SAMURAI* WOULD BE A FOOL TO COME.

SO... WHAT REWARD DID THE CHAMBERLAIN PROMISE YOU ONCE HE BECOMES LORD?
THE CAPTAINCY OF THE GUARDS.
WHAT'S THAT NOISE?
12

KEEKEEEKEEEE

KEEKEEKEEKEEKEE

USAGI--RUN AWAY! OUR LIVES ARE NOT IMPORTANT!
SILENCE!
WHERE'S THE KID?
HE'S ASLEEP IN THE CART.

SEE--I'VE BROUGHT THE BOY...NOW RELEASE THE WOMEN!

YOU ARE IN NO POSITION TO GIVE DEMANDS, SAMURAI!
WAIT--I KNOW YOU! YOU WERE WITH THAT TROUBLESOME INSPECTOR ISHIDA! IS THAT MEDDLER INVOLVED IN THIS, TOO? I SWEAR HE WILL BE PUT TO DEATH!
ESCAPE, USAGI!
QUIET, WOMAN!
13

KILL HIM! KILL BOTH OF THEM!
NO!

YOU'LL BE SAFE UNDER HERE, KOTARO!

GYAR!
URK!

UH!
YAR!
14.

THE KID--! GET THE BOY!
NOW-- WHILE THE SAMURAI IS OCCUPIED!
HIYAHHH!
STOP!

I WILL NEVER SERVE ONE OTHER THAN LORD TOYOFUKU!

EYAH!
15

BAH! THEY CAN'T EVEN HANDLE A LONE SAMURAI!
KOTARO!

I'LL HAVE TO TAKE CARE OF THAT BRAT MYSELF!
NO!

GYAH!
LADY MAPLE--!
STOP!
USAGI-SAN--HELP!
LADY MAPLE--STAY BACK!
URK!

HE'S GOING AFTER THE LORD!
SAVE LORD TOYOFUKU!
MAPLE!

SWISH!
STOP HIM! STOP HIM!
16.

NO, MAPLE--
STAY BACK!
KOTARO IS SAFE!

HHIYAAAAHH!
KOTARO!
I'LL SAVE YOU, MY SON!
LADY MAPLE--
WAIT!

YOU CAN'T HIDE FROM ME, WHELP!
NO!

DIE, BRAT!
17.

KOTAROOO--!
WHA-?!
YOU FOOL!

NO!

LADY MAPLE!

OOK!
MAPLE!
URK!
18

RYAAAAAAAAAAAAHL
GYAH!!

CH-CHAMBERLAIN TOYOFUKU IS... DEAD!
!
B-BUT WHAT OF THE REWARDS FOR LOYALTY WE WERE PROMISED?
COME FORWARD AND I'LL GIVE YOU YOUR REWARDS!
ULP!

THEY'RE RUNNING AWAY. WITH CHAMBERLAIN TOYOFUKU DEAD, THEIR HOPES FOR LATER REWARDS HAVE DIED AS WELL.
ARE YOU HURT, YOSHINO?
N-NO... BUT LADY MAPLE...
19.

HOLD STILL.

ZWIT!!
OH--!

PLOP
PLOP!
PLOP!

LADY MAPLE IS... DEAD.
IT'S MY FAULT!
AT LEAST YOU SAVED--

--K-KOTARO? B-BUT IT'S A-A--
I COULD NOT ENDANGER THE BOY... SO I BROUGHT A DOLL INSTEAD.

LADY MAPLE DIED FOR A DOLL...

NO, USAGI-SAN.
SHE GAVE HER LIFE FOR HER SON.
20.

LATER...
THANK YOU FOR TAKING LADY MAPLE'S BODY AWAY FROM THAT SCENE OF CARNAGE, USAGI-SAN.

HER DEATH WILL BE ATTRIBUTED TO THOSE MYSTERIOUS, HOODED BRIGANDS WHO ATTACKED THE LOTUS HOUSE.
SO HER MURDER WILL HAVE TO REMAIN UNSOLVED.
OFFICIALLY, YES... BUT HER DEATH HAS BEEN AVENGED.

SHE WILL NOT BE LINKED TO ANY CONSPIRACY, AND I DOUBT THAT ANY OF LAST NIGHT'S SURVIVORS WILL REVEAL THEIR PART IN A PLOT TO MANIPULATE THE CLAN'S SUCCESSION.
WHAT OF KOTARO?

HE WILL GROW UP AS AN ORDINARY CHILD... THIS I PROMISE YOU.
JUST AS LADY MAPLE WANTED. MY THANKS, USAGI-SAN.
BUT WHO WILL SUCCEED LORD YAMAHASHI SHOULD HE DIE?

IF LORD YAMAHASHI RECOVERS, HE WILL NAME A SUCCESSOR. IF NOT, THE *SHOGUN* WILL CHOOSE AN HEIR.
WHAT WILL **YOU** DO, YOSHINO? I SEE YOU ARE DRESSED FOR TRAVELING.
THERE IS NOTHING TO KEEP ME HERE NOW THAT LADY MAPLE IS GONE AND KOTARO IS TAKEN CARE OF.

I WILL MAKE THE ONE HUNDRED TEMPLE PILGRIMAGE AND PRAY FOR LADY MAPLE AT EACH STOP.
ADMIRABLE.
21.

GOOD-BYE, USAGI-SAN. I CAN LEAVE KNOWING KOTARO IS SAFE AND IN GOOD HANDS.
REST ASSURED, YOSHINO, HE WILL HAVE A HAPPY CHILDHOOD.

THANK YOU FOR YOUR HELP, USAGI-SAN! PERHAPS WE WILL MEET AGAIN DURING OUR TRAVELS.
I WILL KEEP MY EYES OPEN FOR YOU!

THERE'S ONE MORE THING TO TAKE CARE OF.

GOOD MORNING, ISHIDA.
AH, USAGI! I'M JUST PLAYING WITH LITTLE KOTARO HERE. THERE HASN'T BEEN A CHILD IN THIS HOUSE SINCE OUR OWN SON DIED OF ILLNESS LAST YEAR!
HA HA HA!
I HOPE HE HASN'T BEEN TOO MUCH TROUBLE.
NONSENSE.

WE'RE GLAD YOU BROUGHT HIM OVER LAST NIGHT--THOUGH YOU DID SEEM QUITE AGITATED. I HOPE THERE'S NOTHING WRONG... WELL, BUT YOU DO SEEM TO BE IN GOOD SPIRITS THIS MORNING. ANYWAY, KOTARO IS A WONDERFUL BOY. HIS PARENTS MUST BE VERY PROUD.
HA HA!
22.

ACTUALLY, KOTARO HAS NO PARENTS. I'M GOING TO TAKE HIM TO THE ORPHANAGE. I KNOW THE MATRON THERE...

...UNLESS, OF COURSE, YOU'RE INTERESTED IN--
HA HA! WE'LL GET THE ADOPTION PROCEEDINGS STARTED AS SOON AS POSSIBLE.

HARUKO AND YOU WILL MAKE EXCELLENT PARENTS.
I DON'T KNOW MUCH ABOUT KOTARO EXCEPT THAT HE IS FROM A GOOD *SAMURAI* FAMILY.
HE WILL BE PART OF ***OUR*** FAMILY, NOW.

EXCUSE ME, INSPECTOR ISHIDA, BUT THIS IS A MATTER OF GRAVEST IMPORTANCE!
YES, PATROLMAN?

THERE HAS BEEN SOME TROUBLE AT THE SOUTH *TORII* GATE! CHAMBERLAIN TOYOFUKU HAS BEEN ***ASSASSINATED!***

SIGH! I'D BETTER GO, THOUGH I THINK I'LL TURN THIS OVER TO INSPECTOR NII. HE COULD USE THE EXPERIENCE. BESIDES, I HAD ENOUGH OF CHAMBERLAIN TOYOFUKU IN MY LAST CASE.
I'LL SEE YOU LATER, USAGI.
YOU CAN COUNT ON IT.
23

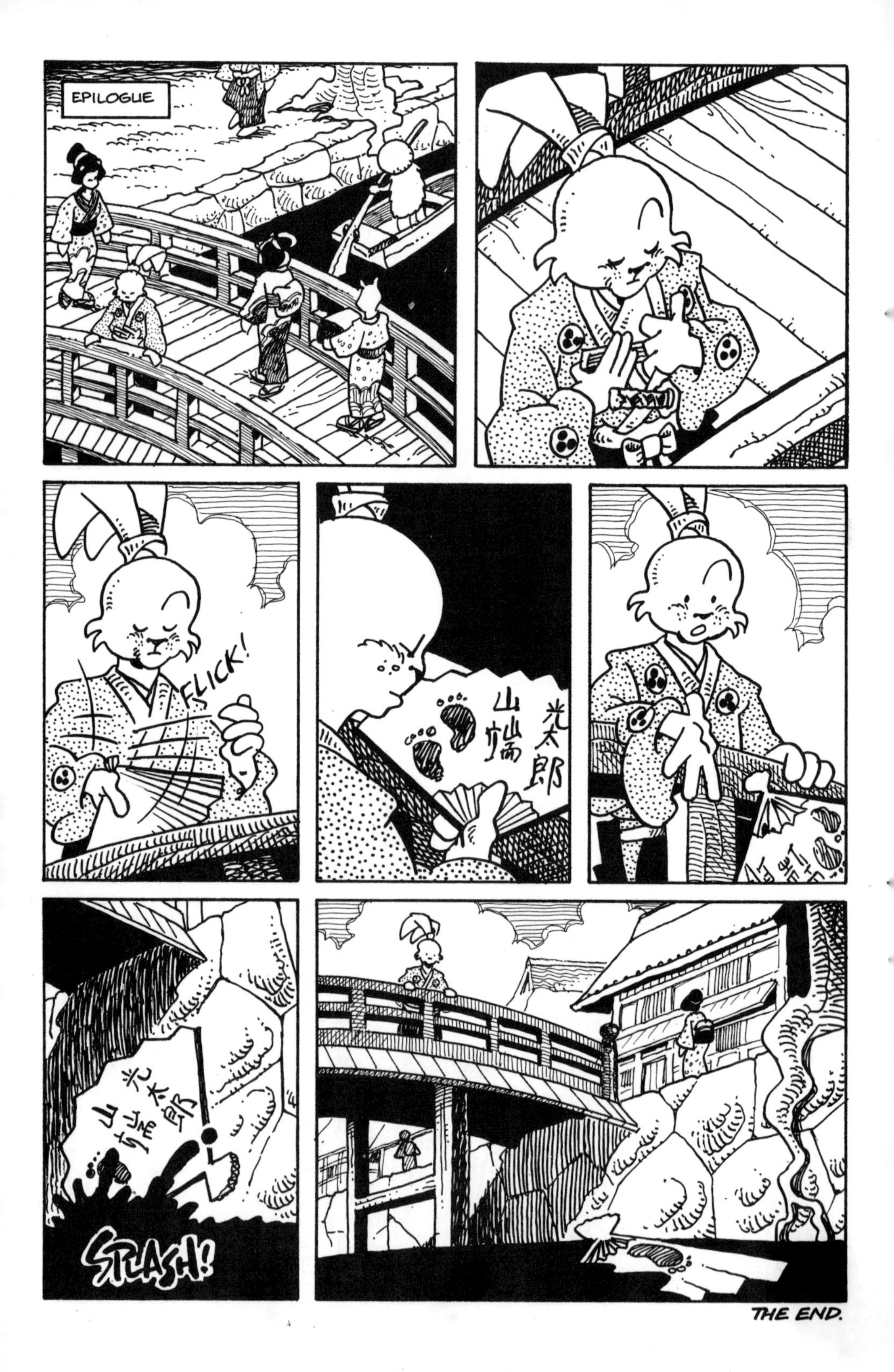

THE END.

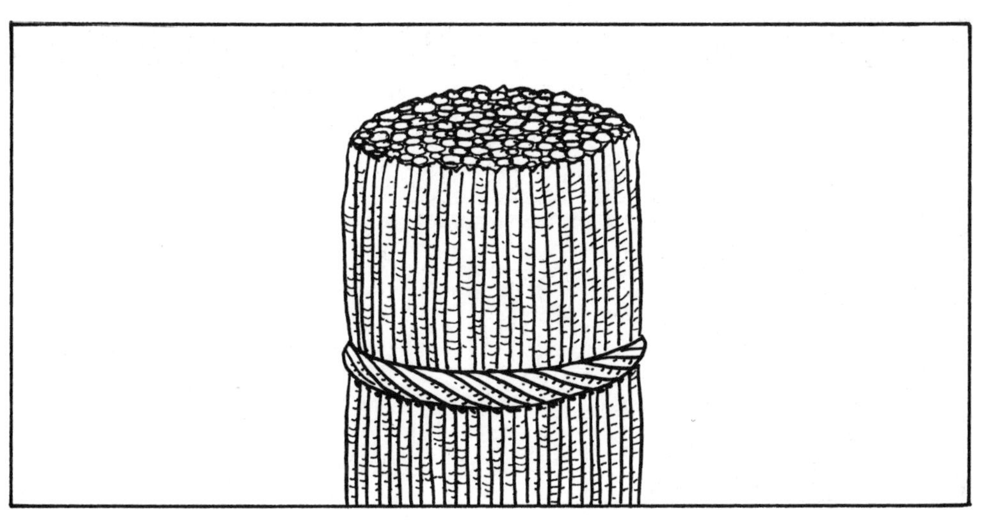

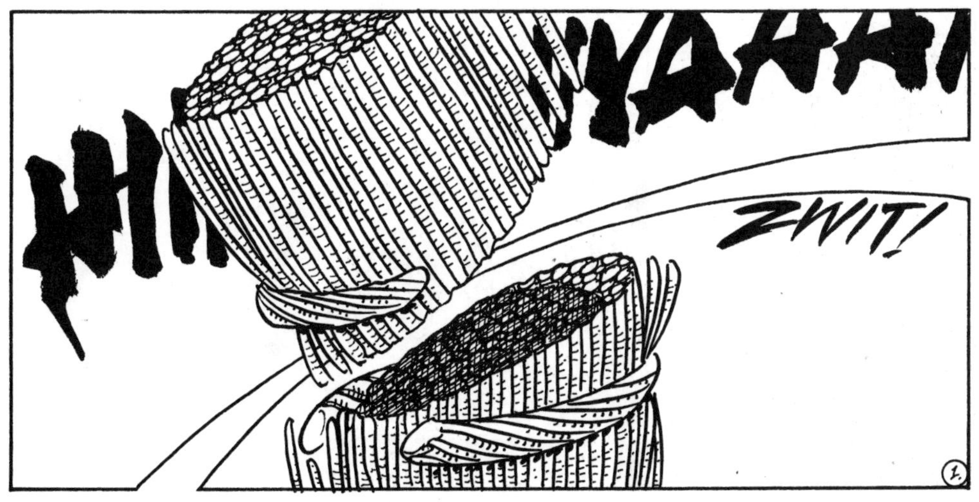
ZWIT!

BAH! ANOTHER POOR STROKE!
YES, SENSEI*!
*TEACHER

DO YOU WANT TO CUT STRAW ALL YOUR LIFE, YOSHII?
I WILL DO BETTER NEXT TIME, SENSEI.

YOU MUST CONCENTRATE! ONLY THE BEST SWORD TESTERS ARE PRIVILEGED TO TRY NEW BLADES ON THE BODIES OF EXECUTED CRIMINALS!
YES, SENSEI.

SUCH TESTING ELEVATES NOT ONLY THE TESTER BUT THE SWORD AS WELL! THOSE BLADES CERTIFIED AS HAVING BEEN TESTED THUS ARE THE MORE COVETED.

NOW SET UP MORE STRAW DUMMIES! REMEMBER-- CONCENTRATE!
YES, SIR!
2

TAMÉSHIGIRI*
AN INSPECTOR ISHIDA MYSTERY
TWENTY YEARS LATER...
HAW HAW! I'LL BE RIGHT BACK!
I'VE GOT TO MAKE ROOM FOR MORE SAKÉ.
HA HA! IT'S NO WONDER! YOU'VE ALREADY FINISHED OFF HALF A BARREL!
I'LL BE BACK SOON FOR THE OTHER HALF!
HA HA HA!
*"SWORD TESTING"

HEY, SAMURAI-- NICE NIGHT, HUH? HAW! HAW!
BURP!

HEY, YA WANNA DRINK, HUH? C'MON, IT'S ON ME! HAW! HAW!

HEY, WHAT'S THE MATTER WITH YOU GUYS?
PUT YOUR SWORD AWAY!
STAY BACK! STAY BACK!

NO! NO!
CRASH!

URK!
ZWIT!

WE CAN'T USE HIM!
THEN WE'LL HAVE TO FIND ANOTHER ONE.
SOMEONE'S COMING!

HEY, BUDDY, WHAT'S TAKING YOU SO LONG?
WHAT'S GOING ON HERE?

COME ON! THERE'LL BE A CROWD HERE IN NO TIME!
OUR ENTIRE NIGHT HAS BEEN WASTED!
HELP! HELP! MURDER!
4

THE WITNESS REPORTED THAT HE WAS KILLED BY TWO MASKED *SAMURAI*.

HAS HE BEEN IDENTIFIED YET?
HE'S JUST ANOTHER NAMELESS PIECE OF SCUM-- PROBABLY GOT WHAT HE DESERVED.
THAT'S **ENOUGH**, OFFICER!
UH... YES, SIR!

TATTOOS... HE COULD HAVE BEEN A PROFESSIONAL GAMBLER.
A VIOLENT LIFESTYLE. COULD IT HAVE BEEN A ROBBERY?
HIS PURSE IS STILL HERE.

A VENDETTA SLAYING?
NO. THERE WOULD BE SOME DECLARATION OF RETRIBUTION.

LET ME EXAMINE THE WOUND.
OF COURSE, USAGI.
5

HMM...
FOUND SOMETHING, USAGI?

HE WAS SLAIN BY A VERY DEFT STROKE. IT WAS NOT AN ORDINARY KILLER.
I SEE... A SKILLED SWORDS-MAN, EH?

A FEW HAVE DISAPPEARED FROM THIS AREA WHICH HOUSES THE LOWER LEVELS OF SOCIETY.
DO YOU THINK THEY ARE CONNECTED TO THIS MURDER?
THEY COULD BE.

BUT THE OTHERS WERE NEVER FOUND.
PERHAPS THAT WOULD HAVE BEEN THE CASE WITH THIS ONE IF IT HAD NOT BEEN FOR THE WITNESS.

THE PROBLEM IS THAT I AM SHORT OF STAFF. MOST OF MY MEN ARE ASSISTING INSPECTOR NII WITH THE ASSASSINATION OF CHAMBERLAIN TOYOFUKU. OTHERS ARE LOOKING INTO THE RAID ON THE LOTUS HOUSE.
HMM... I WONDER IF THEY ARE CONNECTED.
UH... I DOUBT IT.

OTHER OFFICERS WERE AT AN EXECUTION OF TWO CRIMINALS THIS MORNING.
BUT WE'LL FIND THIS MAN'S KILLER.
JUSTICE MUST BE FOR ALL, OR IT IS NOT TRUE JUSTICE.
6.

LATER, AT THE POLICE STATION...
HOW GOES YOUR INVESTIGATION, INSPECTOR NII?
THERE ARE REPORTS THAT A LONG-EARED *RONIN** WAS INVOLVED IN THE CHAMBERLAIN'S MURDER.
WE ARE PUTTING TOGETHER AN ACCURATE DESCRIPTION OF HIM.
UH-OH!
*MASTERLESS SAMURAI
GLBX BLIX!
HE MAY ALSO HAVE BEEN INVOLVED IN THE ATTACK ON THE LOTUS HOUSE. MY MEN ARE SCOURING THE CITY AS WE SPEAK, BUT HE SEEMS TO HAVE DISAPPEARED.
BUT WE WILL FIND HIM, CHIEF INSPECTOR ISHIDA! THIS, I PROMISE YOU!
GULP!
CONTINUE WITH YOUR SEARCH. YOU ARE DISMISSED.
YES, CHIEF INSPECTOR!
GLBT!
HA HA!
7.

THE DESCRIPTION OF THAT *RONIN* MATCHES YOU, USAGI! WHERE WERE *YOU* THE NIGHT BEFORE LAST? HA HA!
ER... YEAH... HA HA UHHH...

SIR! YOSHII, THE SWORD TESTER, IS HERE TO SEE YOU... PRIVATELY.
CERTAINLY. WILL YOU EXCUSE US, USAGI?
I'LL TAKE KOTARO FOR A WALK.

AH, YOSHII-SAN, WELCOME. I GUESS YOU ARE HERE TO INQUIRE ABOUT THE TWO CRIMINALS EXECUTED THIS MORNING.
YES, IKEDA-SAN.
I HAVE A FEW BLADES THAT NEED TESTING.
WHEE! HA HA!
I AM SORRY, BUT YOU MADE THE TRIP HERE FOR NOTHING.

ONE HAS ALREADY BEEN CLAIMED BY YOUR COMPETITORS, THE HAYASHI CLAN OF SWORD TESTERS. THE OTHER CRIMINAL WAS A MURDERER SO IS UNSUITABLE FOR YOUR NEEDS.
YES, WE ARE FORBIDDEN BY CUSTOM TO TEST ON MURDERERS AS WELL AS PRIESTS AND OTHERS.

THE HAYASHI CLAN ALWAYS SEEMS TO HAVE THE PICK OF THE CORPSES.
THIS IS A MATTER YOU SHOULD DISCUSS WITH THE MAGISTRATE. IT IS HE WHO DECIDES SUCH THINGS.
8.

SURELY YOU HAVE SOME INFLUENCE ON THE MAGISTRATE. I WILL MAKE IT WORTH YOUR WHILE...
YOSHII-SAN, I MUST ASK YOU TO LEAVE. IF YOU SPEAK TO ME OF SUCH THINGS AGAIN, I WILL ARREST YOU FOR ATTEMPTED BRIBERY.
"BRIBERY"? I DO NOT SUGGEST SUCH A THING!
BUT I WILL TAKE MY LEAVE IF YOU WISH. GOOD-BYE, INSPECTOR ISHIDA.
GEE! HA HA!
HA HA!
9.

COME HERE, KOTARO!
HE DID NOT LOOK PLEASED.
HA HA HA!
BLIG BLIG!
KLAATU!

YOSHII IS THE HEAD OF THE TETSUMON CLAN, ONCE RENOWNED AS GREAT SWORD TESTERS. HE IS GOOD BUT NOT AS SKILLED AS THE FORMER HEAD WAS, AND THE CLAN HAS SUFFERED A DECLINE.
POO~!

HE NEEDED A BODY FOR TESTING, BUT THE ONLY ONE AVAILABLE IS UNSUITABLE.
HOW SO?
NNNGG!

BY PROTOCOL, THEY CAN ONLY USE EXECUTED CRIMINALS... BUT NOT THOSE WITH SPECIFIC DEFORMITIES, THOSE GUILTY OF CERTAIN CRIMES, OR ETA, THE LOWEST SOCIAL CLASS. THE BODY WE HAVE IS THAT OF A MURDERER AND FORBIDDEN TO THEIR USE.
NNNGH--!

WELL, I'VE GOT TO GET BACK TO WORK. WILL YOU TAKE CARE OF KOTARO FOR A WHILE?
UH...
WAAH!
10.

THAT NIGHT...
¡YAWN!¡ I'VE HAD ENOUGH FOR ONE NIGHT. I'M LEAVING.
WATCH OUT FOR THOSE KILLERS! HA HA!
MAYBE YOU SHOULD WAIT FOR US. YOU'RE SUCH A LITTLE WIMP, YOU MAY NEED OUR PROTECTION! HA HA!
OR MAYBE YOU CAN HIRE A LITTLE GIRL AS A BODYGUARD! HAW!
HAW HAW!

DON'T WORRY ABOUT ME! I CAN TAKE CARE OF MYSELF!
HA! I LAUGH AT KILLERS!

HUH! IMAGINE SUGGESTING I'M A COWARD!
I'LL SHOW THEM! I WISH THOSE MURDERERS WOULD SHOW UP!

BUT IT IS AWFULLY QUIET...
...LIKE A TOMB!

M-MAYBE I SHOULD GO BACK! I--
CRASH!
YAHH!

A TOKAGÉ! A STUPID TOKAGÉ!
SCARED ME HALF TO DEATH!
EEP!
11.

FILTHY BEASTS! THERE SHOULD BE A LAW AGAINST YOUR KIND IN OUR TOWN!
EEP?

DIRTY, FILTHY, ROTTEN BEAST!
CRASH!
EEP!

YEEK! YEEK!
LAUGH AT ME, WILL YOU?! I'LL SHOW YOU!

EEK! EEK!

YOU CAN'T GET AWAY FROM ME SO EASILY!
HA! THERE YOU ARE! I'VE GOT YOU NOW!

ZWIT!
UH--!
12

AN UNSAVORY PART OF TOWN!
WE CALL THIS THE BLEAK QUARTER. THIS IS THE AREA THE DISAPPEARANCES TOOK PLACE IN.
THANK YOU FOR KEEPING ME COMPANY, USAGI-SAN!
NORMALLY MY DOSHIKI* WOULD PATROL THIS AREA, BUT AS I SAID, I'M SHORT-STAFFED.
*PATROLMEN

AND, TRUTH TO TELL, NOT ALL MY MEN CONSIDER THOSE LIVING HERE WORTH THEIR TIME TO PROTECT.

IT'S FAIRLY QUIET TONIGHT.
WORD OF THE DISAPPEARANCES AND LAST NIGHT'S MURDER HAS GOTTEN AROUND. THE PEOPLE ARE INDOORS.
EH?

EEK! EEK!

SOMETHING SCARED HIM!
HE CAME FROM THIS WAY!
13

A PALANQUIN.
IT IS UNUSUAL TO SEE ONE AROUND HERE... ESPECIALLY ONE AS FINE AS THAT ONE.
HOLD IT--WHAT ARE THOSE TWO DOING?
HMM... INTERESTING... USING A PALANQUIN TO TRANSPORT A STRAW MAT...
...AT THIS TIME OF NIGHT.

OOF! THIS ONE'S HEAVY!
THIS WILL BE THE LAST ONE FOR A WHILE.
OF COURSE, THAT ROLLED-UP MAT COULD EASILY CONCEAL A BODY.
CAREFUL WITH THAT, YOU TWO!
HMM... THEY ARE NOT ALONE.

IT'S LOADED IN HERE, SIR!
GOOD. WE DON'T HAVE ALL NIGHT FOR THIS!

14.

HURRY! WE'VE GOT TO GET BACK TO THE TESTING GROUNDS BEFORE IT GETS LIGHT.

YOSHII!
GET BACK BEFORE HE SEES US!

THE SWORD TESTER?
YOSHII COULD NOT GET AN EXECUTED CRIMINAL'S CORPSE, SO HE'S PROCURING HIS OWN! THAT IS WHY THE VICTIM WAS LEFT LAST NIGHT-- HE WAS TATTOOED.
BUT, WHY...

TESTERS MUST OBSERVE STRICT GUIDELINES REGARDING THOSE BODIES THEY CAN AND CANNOT USE-- THEY ARE FORBIDDEN THOSE MARKED WITH TATTOOS.

SHOULD WE STOP THEM?
NO. WE KNOW WHERE THEY ARE GOING. WE NEED MORE OFFICERS TO ARREST THEM!
HURRY!
15

LATER AT THE TETSUMON CLAN COMPOUND...
EVERYTHING IS IN READINESS, YOSHII-SAMA!
EXCELLENT.
WE HAVE FIVE BLADES TO TEST TONIGHT.

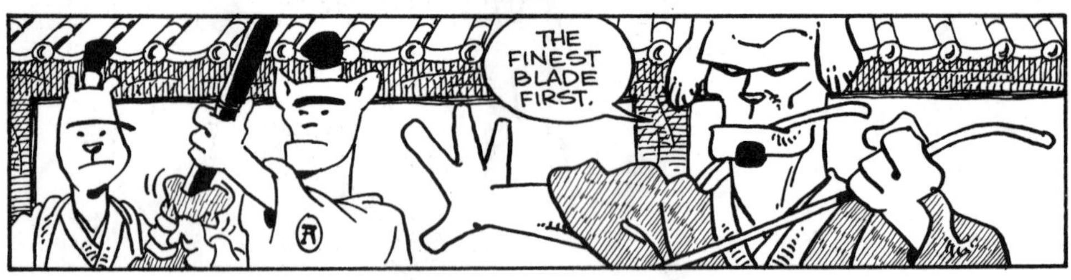
THE FINEST BLADE FIRST.

THIS IS FROM THE SWORDSMITH YAMAHIRA.
FEH! A SECONDARY SMITH.

LET US SEE HOW WORTHY THIS BLADE IS.

SPLOOSH!
16.

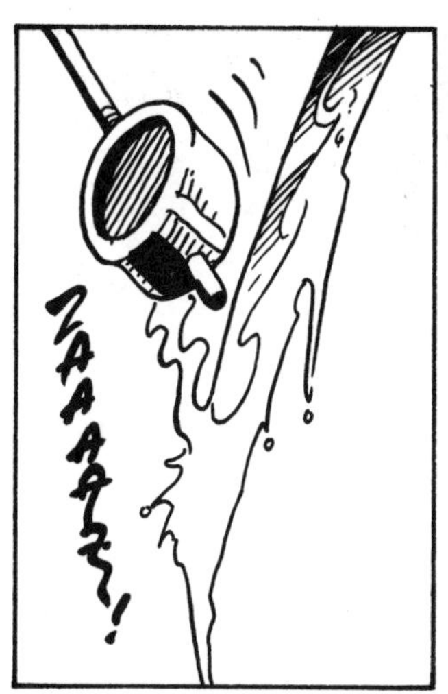
ZAAAAAT!

SPLAT! SPLAT!

ONCE IT IS KNOWN THAT OUR TESTS ARE PERFORMED ON CORPSES, THE GREATEST SMITHS IN THE LAND WILL VIE FOR OUR SERVICES!

I WILL BEGIN WITH THE MOST DIFFICULT OF CUTS--THE *RYO KURUMA**--THEN USE THE OTHER BLADES FOR THE LESSER CUTS.
*PAIR OF WHEELS

YOU SAID, *SENSEI*, THAT MY SKILL WAS FIT ONLY FOR STRAW.
BUT NOW I PERFORM *TAMESHIGIRI* ON A BODY.

I WILL BRING PRESTIGE TO THE CLAN ONCE AGAIN!
17.

HIYAAA

AAAA
STOP!
WHO DARES--?!

YOU'RE UNDER ARREST, YOSHII!
ISHIDA!

DO YOU THINK YOU AND A HANDFUL OF COPS CAN ARREST US?!

SURRENDER QUIETLY, YOSHII, AND PERHAPS YOU WILL ESCAPE THE EXECUTIONER'S SWORD AND BE ALLOWED TO COMMIT *SEPPUKU** TO PRESERVE YOUR LOST HONOR!
*RITUAL SUICIDE

"*OUR LOST HONOR*"?
WE DID WHAT WE DID TO *PRESERVE* OUR HONOR!
18.

MURDER IS NEVER HONORABLE!
WHO ARE YOU TO JUDGE US?!
KILL THEM! KILL THEM ALL!
FOR THE HONOR OF THE CLAN!

URK!
GYAH!
EYAGH!

FLOO--!

UH!

EYAH!
19

CLAK!
HHIYAHH!

SNAP!
OOF!

GYA!
OW!

EYAGH!

HYA!
ARGH!
20.

DIE, ISHIDA!

ZWIIIII...

TANG!
WHA--?!

LEAVE HIM TO ME, INSPECTOR!
SO, SAMURAI, YOU WOULD PIT YOUR SKILLS AGAINST MINE, EH?
TANG!
I HAVE BEEN WITH SWORDS ALL MY LIFE! WHO ARE YOU?--A NAMELESS WARRIOR!

I AM MIYAMOTO USAGI--A RONIN!
A MASTERLESS SAMURAI?! ¡FEH!

WHAT HOPE DO YOU HAVE AGAINST A SWORDMASTER!
21.

YOUR SKILL IS, AT BEST, SECOND RATE, *RONIN*!
ZWIT!

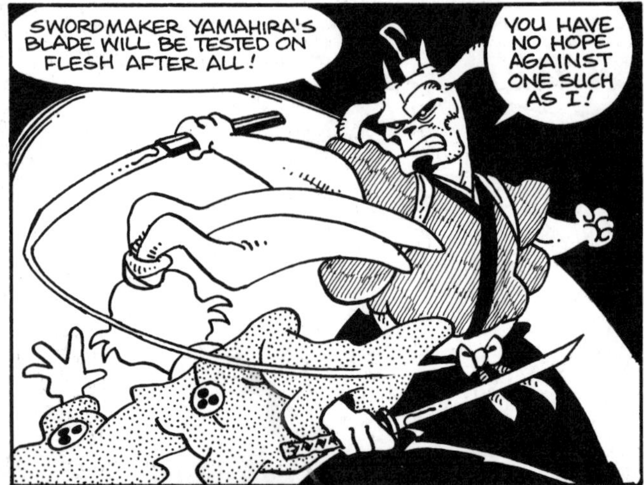
SWORDMAKER YAMAHIRA'S BLADE WILL BE TESTED ON FLESH AFTER ALL!
YOU HAVE NO HOPE AGAINST ONE SUCH AS I!

HHHHHIIIIYAAAA

RRYYAAAAAHH
.....!
22

I-I SORELY UNDERESTIMATED YOU, U-USAGI-SAN...
AH--A MAGNIFICENT STROKE... WORTHY OF M-MY OWN *SENSEI*...
LONG HAVE I WISHED TO POSSESS SUCH SKILL.

BUT... S-*SENSEI* WAS RIGHT...
I ONLY DESERVE TO CUT...
THUD!

...STRAW...

W-WE GIVE UP!
PUT YOUR SWORDS DOWN!
23

LATER...
MUST YOU GO SO SOON, USAGI-SAN?
I WILL MISS YOUR HELP... AND YOUR FRIENDSHIP.
I HAVE ALREADY LINGERED TOO LONG. OTHERS ARE WAITING FOR MY RETURN.
BUT I HOPE WE MEET AGAIN, ISHIDA-SAN, HARUKO... AND ESPECIALLY YOU, KOTARO.

BY THE WAY, IN WHICH DIRECTION ARE YOU GOING?
I'M TRAVELING TO THE NORTH. WHY?
HONK! HA! HA!

WELL, NII HAS NOT YET CAPTURED THAT LONG-EARED ASSASSIN. I THINK HE MAY HAVE ESCAPED TO THE SOUTH. THAT IS WHERE THE SEARCH SHOULD BE CONCENTRATED!
GOOD. I WOULD HATE TO, UH...BE MISTAKEN FOR A COLD-BLOODED KILLER.
BEEP!
HA! HA!

完

Usagi Yojimbo

Grey Shadows Story Notes

The Hairpin Murders

Kabuki was founded in 1600 in Kyoto by Okuni, a priestess of the Oyashiro Shrine in Izumo Province. Her performances were an outgrowth of the *nembutsu odori* (Dance of Prayer to Buddha) and the belief that the principles of Buddhism could be more easily understood through song and dance.

Like many entertainers in Kyoto, Okuni performed on the dry riverbed of the Kamo River. She soon teamed up with Sanza, a *samurai* musician, and together they created dramas and ribald comedies borrowed freely from the *Noh* and *Kyogen* theaters. Okuni would often dress in a man's costume and Sanza a woman's, to the approval of the audience. They soon put together a troupe and went into business for themselves. The needs of the shrine were forgotten, but that's showbiz.

In 1603 this type of entertainment was called *kabuki* (free life).

There were different schools of *kabuki*. The most notorious was the *Yujo* (pleasure-woman) *Kabuki*, in which prostitutes found another means to charm and attract customers. In 1629, all women, in any capacity, were banned from the stage by the Shogun's order, in an effort to protect public morals and limit interaction between the social classes. By banishing women, *samurai* were less likely to attend these shows, which were primarily frequented by commoners. The *onnagata* (female impersonator) was created to offset the boredom of the all-male cast.

I was very lax in historical accuracy in this story. "Narukami" was written well after Usagi's time, but I made reference to it because it is one of my favorites. Also, though Sanza appeared in women's attire, the first true *onnagata* is credited as being Murayama Sakon in 1649.

Sharon and I were in Japan in January of 1998 as guests of Osamu Tezuka Productions. We made a trip to the Grand Kabuki Theatre in Tokyo, though we didn't have the time to actually see a performance. However, we were taken to Takarazuka outside Kyoto to visit the Tezuka museum — an incredible place — and see the Takarazuka Theatre, which is the antithesis of *kabuki* in that all the actors are women. We first saw a historical drama and then a Las Vegas-type show. It was amazing to see the women take on male roles — subtle nuances in posture and the swagger as they walked made them absolutely convincing.

For information on *kabuki* I referred to *Kabuki Costume* by Ruth M. Shaver, 1966, Charles E. Tuttle Co. of Rutland, Vermont, and Tokyo. This is a lavishly illustrated book and is indispensable not only for *kabuki* costumes but for all types of traditional clothing.

The Courtesan

The yearly courtesan procession was a sight to behold. The *oiran*, with her retinue, made an appearance in her finest gowns, walking on foot-high, black-lacquered clogs called *mitsuba-no-kuro-nuri-geta*. Her costume was so voluminous and heavy (fifty pounds or more) that she had to be assisted by one or two *wakaimono* — male servants of a brothel — on whose shoulders she could lean. Her skirts were tied up for easier walking, allowing spectators a view of her bare, white feet. Folded paper peeked out of her collar to be used as a handkerchief. J. E. Becker, in *The Nightless City*, writes: "The sight of a lovely and bewitching *yujo* clad in rich silk brocades glittering with gold and polychromatic tints: of her wonderful pyramidal coiffure ornamented with numerous tortoise-shell and coral hairpins so closely thrust together as to suggest a halo of light encircling her head; and her stately graceful movements as she swept slowly and majestically through the *Nako-no-cho*, must indeed have appeared magnificent and awe-inspiring to the uninitiated."

The *oiran* was a courtesan of high status. The term was supposedly derived from *oira no ane*, or "my elder sister," a term of respect used by apprentice courtesans in the Yoshiwara pleasure district of Edo.

The *oiran* should not be confused with the *geisha* ("art person"), who were women skilled in dancing, singing, playing musical instruments, and conversation. The *geisha* still exist, but the *oiran* as portrayed in period movies and art, have all but disappeared.

There are still processions, however. The *Bunsui Oiran Dochu* in Nishikanbara, Niigata Prefecture, is celebrated usually on the third Sunday in April. The *Senteisai Matsuri* at Shimonoseki, Yamaguchi Prefecture, dates back to the times when court ladies became widows of husbands lost in wars and became courtesans. In sympathy, women don the ceremonial attire to honor them.

The visual for Lady Maple was inspired by the character Agemaki from the *kabuki* play *Sukeroku Yukari no Edozarkura*.

The *torii* is the symbol and gate to a Shinto shrine. The sun is a symbol of Japan, and many early shrines were erected to Amaterasu, the sun goddess. The rooster is associated with the sun. *Torii* literally means "bird perch." A live rooster was placed on a perch as an offering. After time, the perch itself came to symbolize the shrine and represents the division between the everyday world and the spiritual one. Some shrines, such as the Inari Shrine at Fushimi, have so many *torii* that they form long tunnels. The *torii* of the Itsukushima Shrine in Hiroshima Prefecture is regarded as one of the "three great sights" of Japan.

The Yoshiwara District was the licensed "pleasure quarters" of Edo. This was the only area where brothels were permitted in the city, so they could be controlled and regulated. The name originally meant "reed plain," but later the characters used in writing the name were changed, though the pronunciation remained intact, so that the name meant "lucky plain." The area was burnt down at least four times between 1617, the year it was founded, and 1643. As the city spread, Yoshiwara became embarrassingly close to the center, so it was moved to the eastern boundary where it stayed until its dissolution after WWII.

References to this story also came from Ruth M. Shaver's *Kabuki Costume* (which contained a detailed description of a procession and the *oiran*'s costume); *Kabuki: Eighteen Traditional Dramas* by Toshio Kawatake and Akira Iwata, 1985, Chronicle Books of San Francisco (beautiful photographs with summaries of plays); *Japanese Festivals* by Helen Bauer and Sherwin Carlquist, 1965, Doubleday & Co. of New York; *Japan* by Nebojsa Bato Tomasevic, Michael Random, and Louis Frederic, 1986, Flint River Publishers of New York. I also used *Samurai Part II: Duel at Ichijoji Temple*, directed by Inagaki (available on video), which has Miyamoto Musashi staying at the home of a *oiran* on which I based the visuals of Maple's private residence, including that vertically swinging gate. An episode of the *Kage no Gundan II* TV series entitled "The Two-Faces Art of Kunoichi" featured a procession, albeit on a limited production budget.

Tameshigiri

New swords were often tested for strength and sharpness on the bodies of beheaded criminals. The corpses were either suspended from a rope or laid on a mound of sand.

There were eighteen prescribed cuts ranging in difficulty from the *ryo kuruma* ("pair of wheels") across the hips, to the *sodesuri* ("cutting the sleeve") in which a hand was lopped off.

Lesser blades were tested on bundles of straw.